Run Out In The Country

OTHER TITLES

BY RICHARD DIGANCE

Animal Alphabet
Backwater
Another Animal Alphabet

Run Out In The Country

A NOVEL BY

Richard Digance

M
MACMILLAN LONDON

ISBN 0 333 35277 7

First published 1983 by
Macmillan London Limited
London and Basingstoke

Associated companies in Auckland, Dallas,
Delhi, Dublin, Hong Kong, Johannesburg,
Lagos, Manzini, Melbourne, Nairobi,
New York, Singapore, Tokyo, Washington
and Zaria

Filmset in Palatino by Filmtype Services, Limited,
Scarborough, North Yorkshire

Printed in Hong Kong

Contents

— ONE —

From Conception to Toss

Winston Waites, a lithe black lad in his earliest of twenties, travelled with the other multitudes each morning to resume duties as messenger boy/chief cook and bottle washer within the Dickensian office complex of Little & Jackson (Solicitors). He made endless cups of tea, slapped biggish quantities of stamps on biggish-sized envelopes, and stifled yawns from his more than hectic social life. His pocket stereo luckily took the same-sized batteries as his boss's calculator. Roots reggae music clattered and rattled through the discreet earpiece, plastic and blatant white against his tight black curls . . . yet discreet all the same to his work-saturated superiors.

To the astute Winston Waites, a job was a job. He knew well he was one of the fortunate few at Creek Cricket Club who didn't join the job centre queues on Wednesdays. And a job won him admiring glances at the Friday night disco, because it enabled him to afford the trendiest of wardrobes, mustered from the city's finest boutiques. Long-legged Winston rarely walked, more strutted, like an egotistical peacock with the multi-coloured façade of bright satin strides (extra long leg) and size 14½ see-through shirt. It was as though he were a man of rubber, forever chirpy, fingers clicking with the regularity of a Lord's turnstile during a West Indian tour. And in fact the lad strikingly resembled Michael Holding, the great West Indian, whose every ball seemed to enter the earth's atmosphere like a comet before splashing down on off-stump or defensive pad.

Athletic Winston Waites could bowl a tidy over himself, confirming the magnitude of his physique and energy (even if it didn't approach that of the aforementioned). Winston loved the game of cricket; as a matter of fact the only time he wasn't getting his right arm over, he was getting his left *leg* over. Yes, he lived for sport — all sports in general and those two sports in particular. Michael Holding hailed from the exquisite West Indies, Winston from the slightly chillier clime of 24 Priory Road, West Ham, deep in the heart of London's East End. The terraced houses of his road were as plentiful as beach-bound palm trees on the tropical islands, as old and leaning as season-ticket holders beneath the pavilion, as tranquil as a nuclear explosion. The bedroom walls of number 24 trembled to the pulsating rhythms of the sacred stereos (and numbers 22 and 26 seemed to shake in horror too).

Mr Lionel Little, the most senior of the gaggle of solicitors for whom Winston toiled, was close to retirement, and probably closer still to the Great Practice in the Sky. He spluttered often of conscription, the Empire and Tom Graveney, and his absurd inaccuracies were quite, quite charming. He was affectionately known as 'that senile old sod in there'.

Peter Jackson was by many years the junior partner. A young-minded, understanding forty-year old who had passed out at Clare College, Cambridge, with honours and an unexpected century in a Varsity match. His hair was thinning at the nothern frontier of the forehead and his sideburns were no longer in line with his ear lobes. He resided in green-belt Buckinghamshire on a five-bedroomed, six-figure plot on the southern bank of the sedate River Thames, a river reflecting the differing life-styles of solicitor and junior runaround. It was as though the twists and turns, the tides and tumblings had taken the wind from the river's sails. It fairly belted through London's depressed acres, resembling the hapless, hectic cause of its riverside dwellers, racing by, eyes to the front, far too busy to take in the more pleasurable sides of life all around. As an industrial sluggish flow it passed by Winston's friends and neighbours; as a shallow fledgling flow it wandered lazily through the boundary fences of the Little Dow villagers and the boundary ropes of the Little Dow Cricket Club. A long-hop six assured a new ball and a dive for cover from the type of duck not usually associated with the gentleman's game. Peter Jackson captained Little Dow and Winston Waites captained Creek, and that was how the one-day match between the two clubs came to be.

'When Winston started at the office we spoke of law, of cricket, and the laws of cricket. I have to say I was as surprised as the next man that the boss took the lad on, you know, being black and all that, but thankfully it didn't seem to be important to Mr Little. The lad's smile was infectious, he radiated goodwill and humour, and his brother's suit, or 'whistle' as I think he referred to it, almost fitted his lanky frame. I liked him. The office had never been a den of great merriment or chaff, but his smile beamed around us all like Ray East, the Essex slow bowler of local repute, as he closed Little's door at the end of the interview. He had learned of the painfully-slow wicket in Bombay, he had looked agog at his future employer's description of Chandrasekhar's googly, and he had nodded in agreement at the need for more crowd control at the Delhi Stadium. Mr Little spoke of India with great affection; it was a significant part of his beloved Empire. He must have visited the Farozeshah Kotla Stadium, a relic of its own pre-Moghul Empire, at round about the same time as Winston Waites took drags of his first cigarette behind the school bikesheds. We spoke for hours about cricket and occasionally we went over the rudiments of law. We swapped stories and accounts of our favourite innings; quite frankly they were the only accounts the lad understood. The desk-top often became an oaken wicket as marvellous strokes were described. Winston was certainly popular: office girls clamoured for his attentions and the typists often whispered their between-the-sheets fantasies, never realising he had a beautiful black lady who regularly made his back ache, and unaware that the only way to his heart was through an Oval turnstile.

Little Dow Cricket Club, my local village side, were to play Creek Cricket Club, a team of Winston's chums. The date was set for June 16th, a Saturday. It somehow didn't seem six months since the fixture had been arranged and finalised by the two of us. It had been a desperately dull day, shrouded in fog, and Winston and I had sat at the window watching the desperately dull figures setting off on their desperately dull journeys home. Oh, how we all longed for sunshine: the girls longed for Majorca, Mr Little craved for a smattering of four-star Barbados, and Winston and myself longed for a game of cricket, to say nothing of a welcome pint in the afternoon shadows beyond the pavilion. But it all seemed a decade away as we took our umbrellas from the stand like sheriff's deputies raiding the rifle cupboard, accepting the inevitable, our turn to march to the underground station in a sub-zero climate. We spoke of June 16th for weeks after that. It meant a lot to both of us and our attempts at one-upmanship should have brought Stephen Potter rushing to the office to purchase our scripts.

Winston has done well in those six months, you

know. He has successfully negotiated the first few months of a sandwich course at the local college of further education, and last week the rotten bastard cracked a fine century in an hour and a half somewhere near Dagenham. Saturday, June 16th. Christ, that's tomorrow, and yet it seems only the other day I was discussing the new fixture with fellow members of the Little Dow Cricket Club Committee. *Tempus fugit*, does it not?'

Christmas was just around the corner as Peter Jackson, cricket captain, strolled his reluctant canine squatter through the gentle drifts of snow that had been sent on, unwanted, from Berkshire. The Plough Hotel was a welcoming sight, the red glow and applewood log fragrance wafting from public bar to saloon with not so much as a rise in the price. He removed his first three layers of protection as the landlord poured the pint from the wood. The landlord was a tall man, well over six foot, with a roundish pair of shoulders caused by the beams that flashed by each ear as he gathered the empty glasses. In fact, had the ceiling not been raised, he would have been the first man to have possessed a u-bend between the small of his back and the top of his head. Such an odd physical attribute would have caused much grief and consternation had the poor man ever taken a tumble under the influence of his own livelihood. He would undoubtedly rock himself to sleep trying to get to his feet again.

Jackson nodded to other members of the committee as he pulled the minutes and the forthcoming fixture list from his immaculate leather bomber jacket. It seemed strange talking cricket (or Jiminy Rabbit as Winston Waites called it) with frost in the air and snow on the ground. The thatched cottages of the village were as white as a sight-screen, just as though icing sugar had spilled from the church steeple, dispersing in the soft night breeze.

The captain plonked his ale on the top table, pulled his

notes from beneath an Old Spiced armpit, calling order and reaching for an ashtray simultaneously. Pipe-puffing veterans and young hopefuls alike turned to give their utmost attention to the Man of Authority. It fell quiet, but for a stray dart missing its target in the other bar and nestling in the creaking door that separated serious drinkers from serious cricketers. The tired dog yawned beneath the captain's chair, four legs of dog entwined with four wooden legs as it prepared itself for two more hours of human monotone. A saucer of beer would have lessened the boredom, it thought.

Peter Jackson resembled an elongated skybound Derek Underwood on stilts, fair haired and palish eyes, low side-parting, yet nowhere near as low as Tony Lock's. He always wore brown suede shoes and a buttoned cardigan, oozed great contentment, smiled more often than most, and occasionally stunned all those present with a royal blue gag. Young people in Little Dow admired him and his success, old people resented his reluctance to accept middle age.

'Time you knocked all this sporty stuff on the head, what?' suggested one mature specimen.

'Get stuffed!' came Jackson's reply, but nicely. He took his role as club cricket captain very seriously, and responded well to the task.

'Gentlemen, I declare this extraordinary meeting of the Little Dow Cricket Club open. We of course usually start proceedings with apologies for absence, but there seem to be only two people missing this year and neither need apologise. As a matter of fact a letter of thanks from us all may well be in order.'

The huddled sportsmen chuckled at their captain's flippancy and looked around them. Names passed from mouth to mouth until all realised the identity of the absentees.

Archie Metcalf was absent. His brace of mongrels had spent the afternoon at the vets, and they were far too under the weather for the widower to leave. One had felt a nasty jab for hardpad, the other had brought a new meaning to the term 'no balls'. Archie had spent most of his working life as village postmaster, walking the lanes of Little Dow with the regularity that others set their watches to. In winter he cursed his lot, caring not that his footsteps were the first signs of an awakening village in the virgin snow. Despite his occupation, his deliveries on the cricket pitch were tame and tempting to the visiting batsmen. The ball left his palm with the ferocity of a marshmallow, and between the ball leaving him and arriving at the other end, most fielders had ample time to retreat ten or twelve yards from their alloted placements in the field. His sweater had been knitted during the Normandy landings and had turned a gentle hue of buttermilk through the decades . . . it matched the old boy's teeth a treat. According to the agenda he hadn't actually apologised for his absence, but none cared a bean.

Len Wright had dipped out too and that was a different bag of pads altogether. Wright was a stylish bat, quite capable of knocking twenty or thirty without a solitary bead of moisture on the brow. He was in computers, sometimes literally, and spoke of various 'Okey-cokey 200 models' with great authority, though no doubt he could well have fooled all and ignorant sundry with the numerous serial numbers and Japanese consortia that rolled from his silver-forked tongue. He bowled slightly faster than medium, foot-faulting with just about every delivery, not that part-time umpires in loose-fitting decorator's coats would ever have noticed. And so the minute book was opened — apologies accepted or not — to reveal the ups and downs of Little Dow Cricket Club for many years past, its accomplishments and failures, plans long gone and ideas for the future.

Lord Smythe hadn't arrived but wasn't included in the pair. He had rung the Plough, or one of his staff probably had, to apologise for his tardiness. The lord of the manor promised to get to the meet as soon as his talk at the W.I. meeting was over. He was busy fascinating many a female villager with his talk on rearing pheasants, though he probably knew more about blowing their heads off.

Jackson continued. 'We are gathered here, dearly beloved, to renew membership and discuss forthcoming fixtures. It looks like being another hectic season, and I'm delighted to say I've arranged a couple of games with some new opposition. We can't keep on crossing the bridge and playing Swallowfield, Dow Ford and the local public school. I think it would be rather nice to see some new sides coming here to take us on.'

'One of those new sides wouldn't be the police by any chance, would it?' asked Philip Trevelyan, a fine cricketer and sarcastic so-and-so.

'Damn well hope not,' interrupted Joe Baker, opening batsman and honorary treasurer. 'The last time we played that rabble they nicked two sets of pads and John Copeland's box, and we couldn't get the buggers out of the boozer till gone two o'clock.'

John Copeland nodded agreement and took up the story: 'Not only that, Peter, but they were drinking gin and tonics from that box as I was about to pop off home. When I told them it belonged to me they shoved it down my flannels. It stung the old plonker a bit, I'll have you know. I'm certainly well against *that* barbaric tribe coming back.'

Despite Copeland's tragic tale of woe a smile lit almost every member's face. Jackson defused the situation.

'Gentlemen, point taken, I'm sure. Listen, I have no intention of giving the coppers a call. No, not this time. I've plumped for a couple of new sides. Linstone will be here on May 17th for an evening match, and a side called Creek Cricket Club will be playing us on June 16th.

'Who the hell are Linstone and Creek?' asked Geoffrey Baird, a village do-gooder who felt he should know everything that went on in the locality.

'Well,' explained the captain, 'Linstone are a village side from north of Bedford and Creek are from the East End of London.'

'From where?' demanded Baird.

'London. You know London, Geoffrey old boy, it's that great mass where some of us unfortunates have to travel each morning. I work with a young lad who is more than keen to field a side against us on June 16th. I think it's an exciting prospect. They are young chaps, play quite a bit, and should give us a hell of a game.'

'Sounds like a good idea to me, Peter,' agreed Trevelyan. 'What about playing that combined Indian Restaurant side as well?'

'Yes, let's get the Indian wallers down, they bowl far more sensibly than most,' seconded Joe Baker, who welcomed the idea of a side full of slow spinners. A short discussion followed regarding the invention and construction of curried scones and those large crisps the wallers eat with their traditional cuisine, until Jackson considered the chauvinistic chit-chat had gone far enough. He was intent on terminating the meeting as quickly as possible and getting home to bed to assure his boarding of the 7.24 to Marylebone Station.

'Any other business?' he asked.

'Yes, there is as a matter of fact, Peter,' answered the tireless Baker, thus confirming his nickname of Duracell. 'I am damn certain that I've hit upon a good fund-raising idea to raise a few shillings for some new toilets in the pavilion. In this day and age do toilets have to be classed as an unobtainable luxury?'

'What's wrong with pissing in the undergrowth?' asked Trevor White, a remnant of a young hippie. Joe Robbins reconstructed the Grand Remonstrance, well knowing that his wife often tipped the tea leaves behind the pavilion. She was used to seeing nervous batsmen relieving themselves, but her husband thought it a sordid business.

'Is it a reasonable argument to suggest the teapot will not be emptied so frequently behind the pavilion with the installation of a toilet?' he asked.

On this note it was unanimously decided to close the meeting. The landlord had been washing the spent glasses with increasing volume, and the meeting ended on that loud hint. Peter walked the seventy-five yards home to his bed. It was the wrong night of the week so he fell asleep as soon as his pin-striped head hit the pillow and passed into outfields new to dream of wickets and curry and the recurring 7.24.

> 'It hardly seems six months ago, as I say, but Spring had passed, the bulbs had reared their beautiful heads and tomorrow was the day. We'd played four matches, drawn two and lost two, with only Trevelyan and Nicholas O'Connor, a handy medium pacer, showing anything like real form. I walked along the river bank with Stumper, my trusty four-legged friend, rounded the bend upstream of Mrs Pearce's tea rooms (a spot where erosion had widened the river somewhat) and as the brambles and undergrowth disappeared I was suddenly on the outfield of the pitch, a few yards in from the boundary ropes. It was quite late but still light. Anglers unpacked boxes, sandwiches and flasks as they perched by the river awaiting midnight. It would be a big day for them too — the start of the fishing season — at last the chance to come to grips with some early tench or crucian carp. I left them to it and went inland to inspect the wicket.'

Peter Jackson stood at the square for a few moments, taking in all that was beautiful around him. Such a tranquil setting, such welcome peace and quiet for the London commuter. In a matter of hours Little Dow would be taking on Creek Cricket Club. To twenty part-time cricketers it was just another game, but to him and

Winston it was the fruition of many a cold winter discussion at tea breaks various.

Winston tried one more time to win his way with a tasty dancer at the Creek Cricket Club disco. There was always a bit of a do before a game; the players had to check in to discuss availability and team selection, so it seemed a good idea to have a good time while they were gathered together. Three conscientious lads in the far corner discussed the highlights of the Third Test over the vibrant drone of a brass drum keeping time on some alternative record. Medium-pace bowler slapped hands, Jamaica-fashion, with middle-order batsman as each player arrived then sidled off in search of some female accompaniment. Winston and his big brother Rudi arrived at the club after a brisk walk from Forest Gate. Uncool though it sounds, the pair were late owing to domestic chores. Their mother had been widowed by an industrial accident and the devoted sons would never dream of going anywhere until dinner had been prepared, tucked away and digested, with utensils neatly back in place. They were kind lads, tremendously handsome and superstars on the dance floor. Winston was slightly less taller of the two, but his cheery face attracted many inquisitive females, and he loved every minute of it. They arrived together, but an evening was deemed a complete failure if they returned home in the same mini-cab. OK, there was a game on the following day, and it was an eleven o'clock start in Buckinghamshire, but tomorrow was another day.

Rudi had a very round head and full beard, resembling that of the Antiguan pace bowler Andy Roberts, except that Rudi smiled more between run-ups. His sense of dress was immaculate. He danced sparingly, his middle regions rocking to compensate for the rest of his lazy frame. Ladies loved it, however, so he only bothered to gyrate energetically when he was either pissed or stoned.

Brother Rudi was by far the best player in the Creek side; he threw a ball at a batsman with the speed and accuracy of a guided missile and he batted like a possessed American baseball player. He was six foot three inches tall, and though he had played in minor Essex leagues he preferred to be the mighty fish in the smallest ornamental bowl. His Caribbean shirts, replete with yachts, palm trees and well-bodied ladies were as loud as brother Winston's stereo. A bad knock to him was twenty to thirty runs without a six in the dismal process.

Rudi hadn't worked for over four months and envied Winston his job at Little & Jackson's. His long legs always led him to the notorious queues on Wednesday mornings for despite obtaining CSEs in Use of English and Woodwork, vacancies for essayists on sideboards were few and far between. No, Rudi was more than a little stymied, and well he knew it. In quieter moments he kicked himself for never attending the various Essex county trials which had been arranged on his behalf by a considerate sports master. He could have been on television every Sunday rather than in the queue every Wednesday. To console himself, Rudi scored with two girls, so Winston did the brotherly thing by taking one of them home. Nothing wicked ensued, just a little necking and pecking on the balcony of the council flats. After all, she was Screwball Pinder's younger sister, and the two lads were playing cricket together the next morning.

Peter Jackson yawned deeply while his dog relieved itself at deep mid-wicket. He looked south towards the sluggish River Thames, the wicket behind him. Oak trees lined the distant bank like oversized fence supports, their branches steady in the still air. To his right stood the very rustic pavilion, which will be described in great detail a little later because it is in need of further attention. To his left he spotted a couple of figures in the distance. A faint sound of bat on ball filtered through the nets in the furthest corner, on the edge of Lord Smythe's estate. The captain went on his way to identify who was keen enough to practise his strokes on the eve of an important game. He strolled round the square and on towards the far boundary in the general direction of the practice nets. Stumper hated lengthy walks and his body truculently performed four different movements to clear his four legs over the one-inch boundary rope. On plodded man and dog, one speedily, the other reluctantly, towards the players in an elliptical path across the extremes of the outfield. The dog fancied another strain but he knew a second drain-out would culminate in an almighty smack round the muzzle in front of the disgusted on-lookers, so he chose not to bother. It was Geoffrey Baird, his son David and an unfamiliar lad at the bowler's stump.

'Evening, Peter old man, how's tricks?' said Baird.

'Fine, just fine, Geoff. Getting some last-minute practice in, are we?'

'Well, we thought we might as well. David's just got back from university, and in the hope of being chosen for tomorrow's game he's decided to have an hour in the nets. Keen these youngsters, Peter. He hit two centuries for his college during term. Should be good for fifty tomorrow, I reckon,' hinted Baird.

Peter merely nodded politely, never having been that struck on the nosey parker. Certainly he had never intended Baird's unbearable boy to be included in the Little Dow squad.

Baird senior tossed a sitter to Baird junior, who proceeded to crack the gift of a delivery halfway back to his university campus. The ball screamed along the inner net on direct line for Jackson's head.

'Bloody hell, I felt that go by,' complained the disgruntled skipper.

'Should have caught it then,' the student giggled as the ball raced towards the river, flying past the dog shit before coming to rest in the matted dying daffodil undergrowth between oak and elm.

'Fetch, boy!' commanded the pointing master to the unimpressed hound who looked up with a 'Piss off and get it yourself' look. Nobody gave chase, bar the young stranger who knew the recovery of the ball meant at least one bowl at the wicket as a prize for his efforts. Off the lad sprinted, his twelve- or thirteen-year frame unabused by beer, fags or idleness. Geoffrey and Peter turned to discuss the neatness of the wicket, though little could really be determined from such a distance.

'Batsman's wicket that, Geoffrey old boy,' bluffed Jackson, knowing that there was a 50/50 chance he would be right, 'and they're a damn good batting side. Wouldn't surprise me if they cleared four hundred on a strip as kind as that.'

It was very early to allow for pathetic bowling performances from his side, but Peter thought he might as well get started as Baird was there to take it all in. He did, too, nodding his head in ignorant agreement.

'Reckon you're right there, though I'd be more surprised if we knock up four hundred and one and win the bloody game, what?'

The pair mechanically flung their heads well back and roared with laughter. Meanwhile, the young lad had returned with the much-travelled ball, half returning it, half holding on in the hope of a bowl at the stumps.

'Go on, sonny, bowl at my David,' offered Baird condescendingly. The young legs strode up to the single stump at the bowler's mark and a delivery of perfect line and length skittled the middle stump backwards to the rear of the nets.

'What a beautiful ball,' commented Jackson.

'Well bowled, my lad,' seconded Baird.

'You clever bastard,' muttered the defeated young batsman out of adult earshot.

Peter walked across to the boy as David Baird rescued the stump and knocked it back into the ground with the end of his bat.

'What's your name, son?' he asked.

'Tom Tarry, sir.'

'That was one hell of a ball, Thomas, try another?'

'Yes, sir. Oh and it's Tom not Thomas.'

The ball was tossed into left palm from right, then from right palm to left as the youngster waited for the batsman to take up his precise stance. Tarry took just the one step this time. It was a somewhat shorter ball, turning slightly to leg, and caught the unfortunate batsman in no man's land. The ball walloped David's front pad and it was plum LBW.

'Damn fine ball, Tom,' congratulated Jackson.

'Unlucky lad, good try,' came the natural response from the father defending his batting son. There was no doubt that David Baird was a fine cricketer of immense promise, scoring regular runs at university level, yet twice he had been outplayed by the mastery of the younger bowler. He well knew it was LBW, even though he preferred to accept his father's word as gospel. Tom Tarry had outwitted the lad twice with consecutive balls and neither Baird junior nor senior were impressed. Peter Jackson strolled over to Tom, accepting the ball the lad offered, and he too tossed it from one palm to the other.

'Bowl regularly, Tom?' he asked.

'No, not really. Never had the chance.'

'Where are you from? I don't think I've seen you around the village before,' the captain continued.

'We've just moved into the workhouses behind the wall over there,' explained the youngster, pointing to the huge brick barricade that separated ordinary humble human beings from the kingdom of Smythe.

'What are you doing for his worship then?' asked Baird senior with more than a trace of sarcasm.

'I'm the new gardener's assistant, and general run-around, I s'pose,' Tarry admitted, as though confessing to some sort of crime in the dock.

'Oh really, that's interesting, isn't it?' Baird responded.

'Of course it ain't,' Tarry remarked abruptly, 'but I ain't got no exams, 'cause me old man booted me out of school a bit sharpish. S'pose I'm lucky to have any sort of job at all. Anyway, I've gotta dash, thanks for the bowl, sir,' Tarry said as he half-bowed and turned away towards the rich man's fortress. Within thirty seconds he was well into the outfield, stepping out smartly, and not a single word had been spoken by the three who remained. The village cricket captain gave chase, calling to the boy in one tone, and to his lazy dog in another.

'I say, Tom!' yelled the panting runner, 'I say!' Tom Tarry, ignoring the first call but responding to the second, turned about as if on parade, and waited, hands in his pockets, as Jackson approached with the all-too-familiar stumblings of a beer-bellied wicket-keeper shuffling to long leg to save a solitary bye. 'I say, Tom old boy, now look here, you look quite a classy player to me. I couldn't care one iota if you're a gardener's mate or a bloody prime minister, I'm always on the lookout for good young cricketers. How would you like to play for Little Dow tomorrow against Creek?'

Tarry shrugged his shoulders. 'I don't think so, sir.'

'Why on earth not? Oh and it's Peter Jackson, not sir.'

'Well, put it this way, Mr Jackson, I wouldn't mind a game because I've never played in a proper game before, but I ain't got nothing to wear, d'you know what I mean? I'd be nervous an' all, thinking I might let you down.'

'Never you mind that, young man, you be at the pavilion at ten-thirty and for all I care you can play in your damn dungarees. OK?'

'OK, Mr Jackson, oh . . . and thank you very much.'

The two sportsmen nodded to each other and Jackson wandered away trying to guess the boy's age. He looked only twelve or thirteen but he must have been sixteen, maybe seventeen. He came to the conclusion that not only did the lad need cricket flannels, but a hot bath and a square meal too.

'Not a bad cricketer that one, Peter,' commented Geoffrey Baird.

'Quite agree, quite agree,' Peter agreed. 'Matter of fact he's playing tomorrow.'

'Oh I *am* pleased, that's good for the lad,' remarked Baird.

'Yes but it's not too good for your lad I'm afraid, Geoffrey old boy, he's now twelfth man.' The Baird pair's faces dropped like the rain at Old Trafford as Jackson turned away towards the river with Stumper close on his heels. He chuckled mischievously, not daring to turn his head. Stumper stopped to have a quick sniff at what was his anyway but Jackson walked on, keen to get back to write out the new batting order. It was a good week for the captain, being able to select eleven from twelve instead of the usual eight. At home, Stumper spat and splashed his way through a bowl of water while Peter sat down at his bureau with a gin and tonic and a notepad. For no apparent reason he developed a slight headache so went to bed.

'I felt much better when I woke at seven-thirty. My fat lump of a dog was still sound asleep on the kitchen floor so that spared me another energy-sapping stroll. My dear wife had whitened my boots and keeper's pads, I noticed, while I searched every drawer in the sideboard for the wretched scorebook before remembering that Aubrey Padgett had taken it home to update the previous game in his fine italic hand. I pulled back the velvetine lounge curtains and a brilliant shaft of sunlight caught me right between the eyes. I stood with the curtains either side of me like an actor staring into the follow-spotlight in the first scene. It was a timely opening because the sky was hardly the clear blue ceiling I had been anticipating. Grey then white clouds jostled for placings as they raced across the open air in the wake of a still morning breeze. There were few blue holes through which the sun could peep, but there it was just the same. The sun had got its cricket hat on, hip hip hip, hooray!

I whistled a happy tune, no not that one, and inhaled deeply even though the glass of the patio door separated me from the crisp air. I felt weary; I always felt weary on a Saturday morning, but I chose not to sleep late despite the fatigue and the build-up of sleep in my eyes. Time was far too precious if I was to get to the Oxford sports shop and return in time to meet young Winston and his lads as they arrived at the meadow.

I was in the old motor quite early to shoot into town and returned with a cricket bag full of white goodies for my new star. There were flannels (I hoped they would fit) a sparkling white shirt and a white sleeveless jumper with red and yellow piping. Boots were a problem because I hadn't the foggiest idea what size the lad took, so I bought a couple of pairs of tennis shoes, the shop assistant very kindly offering to refund me on the pair that didn't fit. Tom Tarry was all set. It had cost a fair few bob but I didn't mind. It was to be one hell of an occasion for the boy.

I remember searching out the lad on the other side of 'the wall'. His was a minute one-up, one-down workers' cottage, about twenty foot square, flush against the boundary brickwork. The village clock was striking nine-thirty by the time I knocked on his door. It was opened immediately and Tarry looked confused as he recognised my face — perhaps he had been dropped, perhaps Lord Smythe didn't want one of his peasants to turn out for the same side as himself? I glanced into his one downstairs room. There on the sofa was a bright new pair of cricket boots, still without laces, some old yellow trousers with matelot flairs and a khaki safari shirt. The lad had tried to approach the regulation white strip. Little did he know.

In fact Lord Smythe, who we called Smutsy, had no

idea his worker was playing until they collided at the pavilion, but Smythe was hardly one to care. Although he was all hacking jacket and trout flies on the outside, deep down he was a placid character who had made his fortune much earlier in life on the Stock Exchange. His life revolved around dinner parties and game shooting. His weekly game of cricket was his token turn-out with members of the village. He owned the pitch, too, but had donated it to the cricket club with the unofficial rider that he played when he wished and that he always flung down the final over. It was the least we could do to reciprocate his generosity. He certainly would have raised no objection about playing alongside young Tom Tarry. Indeed, if he even knew who Tom Tarry was. After all, I doubt they had ever met.'

Rudi Waites awoke bleary-eyed, in somebody else's arms, in somebody else's bed-sitter. It certainly had been quite a party judging by the empties strewn across the floor, which resembled the Hill at Sydney a hundred minutes after the toss.

He knew it was time for getting up though he felt more like throwing up. He searched hard for his underpants and the name of his bed mate, and walked across to the bedroom window, screwing his eyes up to shut out the trespassing sunlight. He hoped the view would reveal his whereabouts and that the short stroll would clear his head, but neither had the desired effect. He searched for the time but the only hands in the room were of the groping variety, and redundant now. His head pounded like a reggae bass drum and his mouth felt like the bottom of a birdcage. He returned T-shirt and pumps to their rightful stations and tiptoed round the room in search of additional togs. What with the current weather conditions the game of cricket would obviously go ahead, so there was little chance of nipping back between the sheets. A unique case of 'Sun stopped play'.

He found his jeans in the bathroom and his underpants at the bottom of his bed. There was a mop of crazy-coloured hair and a trail of mascara on the pillow. Rudi departed quietly through the front door and broke into an easy jog along Ilford High Road towards his mother's house. The scratches down his back were already smarting as his tee-shirt rubbed on the embossed souvenirs of the night before.

Winston had done the brotherly thing and sorted the various flannels and shirts from the airing cupboard. Winifred Waites had gone about her duties as school cleaner at the local comprehensive, a chore she enjoyed more on a Saturday than during the week, when hundreds of kids clomped across her polishing. Saturday was chin-wag day with the other chars. Winston had packed the Tesco plastic bags and sat awaiting the return of randy Rudi. He saved a burnt offering from the electric toaster, scraped off the top layers and chewed on the remainder, a sound unkind to his delicate head. Rudi raced in, took a quick shower and within ten minutes the two were hot-footing it down to the Waggon and Horses in the Romford Road where the team had agreed to muster for transportation to the new world that was Buckinghamshire. Winston had a gut ache, and belched helplessly into the morning air. He had been drinking Tequila Sunrises the previous night, but the inexperienced barmaid — well, inexperienced at mixing cocktails at any rate — had completely loused it up, offering a dubious fluid that could be more accurately labelled a Bethnal Green Total Eclipse of the Sun. The geographical error was playing havoc with Winston's innards and it was far too early for the hair of the dog. A nine o'clock departure had been arranged and Winston wanted to be the first arrival considering he was skipper. Not that he was . . .

Eddie Peters had arrived with two hours to spare. He loved fiddling with his car, which was just as well because his '68 Consul was falling apart. Eddie had decided to treat his mechanical mate to an oil change in preparation for the long trek to Little Dow, and living on the third floor of a council block he thought the forecourt of the pub was a pretty decent venue for the mucky operation. Luckily the landlord slept soundly, or Eddie would have landed himself in the nearest casualty ward. His legs had disappeared beneath the chromed chassis, but Winston recognised the wheels and the red and yellow running shoes immediately.

'Eddie's here,' he told Rudi, pointing to the running shoes. 'That's three of us and one jam-jar. Not a bad start, eh?'

'Right on, brother.'

Vince Clayton and Julian Jannik rolled up in Clayton's dad's Ford. The two passengers were not the best of friends it must be said, but they lived in the same road and slept with the same fun-loving girls. Clayton was blacker than the rest, his African features far more prominent than those whose ancestors had paddled from the West Indies. He had six or seven deep furrows on his forehead that probably could have yielded broad beans if they'd been filled with potting compost. His eyes shone bright white, perfectly round and darting. He was a superb batsman who, like Tony Greig, could never find a bat large enough to complement his massive physique. A splendid figure in his herringbone suit and open-necked shirt, Clayton looked famous for some strange reason, and yet for an even stranger reason he wasn't. He was not an intelligent man, but scored heavily with the attributes he did have.

The three chums shook hands while the quiet Julian Jannik locked the motor before assisting Eddie with his oil change. Julian was very much an unknown quantity and, looking remarkably similar to Winston and Rudi, had often been mistaken for brother number three. Like his hero Joel Garner he spent hours birdwatching, so looked forward to this excursion to the countryside. He hoped to sight a kingfisher on the unspoilt banks of the river, but failing that he would be more than happy with five or six wickets.

The third vehicle of the entourage arrived, laden down with superfluous headlights and other chrome accessories, and by ten minutes past nine the excited cricketers set off for Buckinghamshire. They laughed and joked away a few miles like overgrown schoolboys, discussing the previous night's better points, while Slogger Stevenson, who had already undertaken a particularly heavy milk-round that morning, slept peacefully in the back of one car. The motorcade threaded its way along the embankment and on to the motorway towards Jackson's village.

'I've just bought my old lady a parrot.'

'Yeah, why's that, man?'

'Well, she said she likes a cockatoo.'

One car load chuckled, another bunch helped the driver with his navigational deficiencies and the third sat intently listening to Rudi's account of his delightfully tiring night.

It was a journey of about an hour and a half, including a few minutes for the weak-bladdered to regain their comfort. Twenty minutes before the start of play the three cars rattled and battled their way into the outskirts of the village.

'Where's the bleedin' pitch then, Eddie my son?' asked Stevie Whiteman.

'How do I know, you berk!'

'Look, there's an old dear there. Stop and ask her where the cricket pitch is, Eddie,' suggested Pumps Parker, an ambulance driver by trade, an ambulance driver's cargo by nature. He was excellent at table tennis and snooker, passable at darts ('arrows' as he called the game) but Winston Waites could sum up his cricketing prowess in two simple words:

'Fucking useless.'

The leading vehicle screeched to a halt a few feet beyond Lily Grace, a most upstanding woman of the parish, a local councillor and treasurer of the Women's

Institute. The two followers skidded and slid in behind, causing house martins and swallows alike to clear off for safer nesting locations. A cloud of cigarette smoke (smoke with a rather pungent aroma) billowed into the sky like steam from an empty radiator as Rudi Waites rolled down the window.

'Excuse me, darling, where's the cricket?' enquired the captain's brother.

'Probably in the grass. Why, can't you hear him chirping?' retorted the smart lady.

'Not *that* cricket, the *game* of cricket. Can you tell us where to go?' he continued.

'Come on, you old bag, or we'll be late,' muttered Alfie Donald to the tweedy lady of River Tweed proportions.

'Leave it out,' whispered Rudi, 'or she'll have you for her bleedin' breakfast.'

'Young man, if I had that little scoundrel for my breakfast I would ensure a spittoon was near to hand. Left at the public house, down to the river and you will see the cricket pitch on your right. Switch off your engine and leave the car tucked just off the footpath. You'll have to walk the rest.'

'Cheeky cow, who does she think she is?' asked the despondent skipper who hated walking anywhere.

'I heard that, young man, and if it will put your mind at rest let me tell you right now that I am one of the umpires for your cricket match.'

'Shit!' remarked Winston.

'We might as well go home now,' suggested another.

Lily Grace enjoyed the cross banter, she had a part-time, but sharp, sense of humour and grinned as the three cars turned left in the distance. The visitors cursed their own lippy demands for directions, knowing it was worth a couple of LBW decisions to Little Dow. Lily Grace loved cricket, had a fairish idea of the rules and longed to put the wicked East Enders in their place. Most certainly a case of the umpire strikes back.

The Little Dow wicket was a sight to behold, a setting of tranquil beauty nestling beside the banks of the river. Trusty oaks and elms lined the boundary adjacent to the river, but not parallel to it. If one was standing by the river bank, the parade of trees would shoot away at approximately thirty degrees to one's right. Directly ahead stood the eighteen-foot-high wall that assured Lord Smythe's seclusion (though it has to be stated that most of the Creek players had scaled walls twice that height at various football grounds around the country). To the left was the pavilion. The trees threw welcome shadows across the outfield for ageing boundary fielders and mad dogs to shelter from the mid-day sun. The sun was scarcely shining yet, though it hadn't actually rained (which was lucky considering that Eddie Peters' car didn't possess expensive extras like windscreen wipers, or indeed a roof).

The wicket was exactly twenty-one yards in length, an intentional shortcoming that allowed the blame to be passed on for over-pitched deliveries that had been hammered on the half volley to various parts of the boundary. A slight incline from Lord Smythe's fortifications to the river bank would have been blatantly visible from the rickety pavilion, had its steps not lilted to blend in with nature's very own inaccurate spirit-level. The red-bricked wall stood splendid beyond the far boundary rope. The gates bowed down from the supports in an arched design, the top of the structure culminating in a gigantic semicircle when the gates were locked. Mature shrubs stretched up the wall with the more capable ivy climbers, like suicidal mountaineers on a sheer-faced route. Graffiti was minimal, because night-time lovers had been far too busy to etch their initials and messages on the discreet wall that sheltered their secret cuddles from the prying eyes of late dog-walkers.

True, it took a good eye to notice the leaning meadow, and Rudi and Winston had spotted it the moment they alighted from the car, but such good eyes had not appeared on the scene since the late, usually very late, Ossie Trentham departed from the village in particular and the world in general with a few magnificent centuries under his belt. A prodigious batsman was Oswald, managing to clout four balls into the lord's acreage beyond the redbrick wall each season. The kind Ossie had left the club enough cash in his will to enable them to erect a fine wooden bench directly in front of the pavilion steps. The bench was inscribed:

In memory of a beloved Ossie Trentham 1898–1974.
Bowled at last.

He was a fine opener, Little Dow's greatest to this day. He had been set to join Worcestershire, but owing to disagreements in Europe had ended up in the trenched mud-baths of France halfway through the First World War. Captain Trentham was never one to show remorse, and as long as he remained on the winning side that was all that mattered to him. Unlike the legendary Charles Burgess Fry he never cared for the title of Captain, Ossie was good enough.

The lads pulled their bags from the trio of car boots and looked around them like released prisoners experiencing the joys of freedom once more. Julian marvelled at the singing birds overhead as Winston led his team across the right-hand side of the outfield. Little Dow's side and its spectators stared at the healthy-looking posse of East Enders as they approached. Young men like Vince Clayton and Julian Jannik looked frightening to the middle-class middle order of Little Dow, who were soon to realise that cricket was not confined to medium-pace bowlers and pot-bellied batsmen. As the eleven alien figures strolled over from the elderly vehicles parked at random, the very size of them drew superlatives from the waiting home side.

Peter Jackson broke away from the gaping on-lookers

and met his office junior by the boundary. There were friendly smiles from Winston and his lads, then eleven voices answered Jackson's query regarding the trip up from London. Winston peered at the gathering and winked at his brother as a gesture of immense confidence. The home captain led the visitors to their changing room, a small area for such huge men. Allotment tenders behind the pavilion rested on forks and shovels and also stared at the new arrivals. Wood pigeons landed by french bean lines, pecked at the luscious leaves, then zoomed off without the gardeners noticing a thing. They victory-rolled before settling on high branches of the oak trees at the other side of the ground, ready to catch at least half a dozen overs before taking off again. When the week-end diggers spotted the chafered leaves they blamed the slugs. As the travellers rinsed their faces with cold water to prepare for the game, the gardeners rinsed their soil with salt water to disperse the slithering but innocent trespassers.

Rudi rolled a mixture of Lebanese and Old Holborn and passed it around the room while brother Winston set off for the wicket with Peter Jackson, his boss and rival captain. Work was never mentioned as they walked the fifty yards; Jackson thought much better of it and Waites thought of much better things. The rain was holding off but it was still overcast. The visitors' changing room echoed with laughter. The home side's changing room was as quiet as a graveyard as eleven determined men changed into their whites, scared witless by the size of the enemy.

The crowd arrived in twos and threes, welcomed with the same remark.

'My god, you should see the size of them.'

'How long have they been here then?'

'Don't rightly know, but you should see the size of them.'

Some young village girls raised their eyebrows in expectancy giggling at the thought of such talent in their midst. It was two minutes to eleven o'clock. The game would start on time if Aubrey Padgett was able to speed up the process of entering the two sides into the scorebook.

Slogger Stevenson always opened the batting for Creek. He was a foundry worker at Ford's and had arms like telegraph poles. He was a meagre five foot eight inches but well built all the same. His highest score was three go-go dancers in one long, exotic night. On the cricket pitch he had once hit a remarkable 174 against Parkside Old Boys and won the man of the match award, as well as a side bet he'd had with Rudi Waites that he'd get into double figures. He wore distinctive yellow cords, tight fitting around the crutch. Occasionally, in less important fixtures, he wore his jock-strap on the outside. He was a dab hand at the square cut for four runs, and did a bit of shoplifting from time to time. His headband concealed his ancient Beatle hairstyle, but Slogger never bothered about such things. He certainly didn't want to know about a poncey protective helmet or an even poncier white floppy hat.

As a rule, the opening partnership was completed by the unpredictable and pathetic *Eddie Peters*. He was mainly there to lull the opposition into a false sense of security before Clayton smashed them all round the ground at number three. Trying to emulate Bill Lawry, Eddie once batted for two and a quarter hours for a paltry seven runs, before being given out LBW by an umpire with an unfortunate bowel complaint.

Vince Clayton, the black, frowning number three had been brought up on Keith Boyce, having studied his style for hours at Ilford's Valentines Park. Rumours had flown hither and thither regarding the lad's physique. Wide-eyed females ogled him incessantly at the disco from the waist down, and his protective box had once been second prize in the Creek Club's Christmas raffle.

After Clayton, assuming somebody took his wicket,

came *Screwball Pinder*, and a more extreme opposite to Clayton could not be found. Screwball could certainly not boast such magnificent attributes. He was pale and ginger and Irish-looking, but sadly lacking in shamrock wit. His most outstanding feature was his concave chest and his disregard for cricketing traditions. For instance, he never took guard, preferring to puff on a fag until he reached the crease. It was as great a ritual as Boycott tipping his cap before a delivery except that Boycott never got through as many caps as Pinder did cigarettes. Screwball (real name Walter) cleaned the pavilion back in the Far East End and could always be blamed in defeat. He was an ignorant whipping boy and yet seemed to enjoy the role.

At five and six came Rudi and Winston respectively and number seven went to *Stevie Whiteman*, the only slowish bowler in Creek's side. Stevie never grew up, at twenty-five he still felt more secure in the company of teenagers or thereabouts. He forever loafed in black cords — cricket matches, weddings, funerals, it really made little difference — only the depth of the crease changed to suit the particular occasion. Poor Stevie had a drink problem too, and once, when umpiring in a match with Manor Lodge 'B', he gave four LBW decisions in a single over before being sent back to the pavilion. He loved his booze and tolerated everything else.

Spectacular *Montgomery Holt* owned the ugliest car in London and batted number eight. A chrome-laden beast of a Zodiac resembling a nomadic outbuilding more than a motor, it was Monty's prized possession. He was a positively tasteless chap, sporting his very own keeper's pads dyed in the sacred colours of claret and blue. Yet he kept wicket with a certain panache, not a Godfrey Evans clone (except in the betting shop) rather a pastiche of Farooq Engineer as he dived backwards and forwards. Monty often gave oncoming bowlers migraines with his dazzling pad movements. He thought backward short-leg was a reference to some stupid jockey or other and his greatest feat during a game was to eat twenty-five egg and cucumber sandwiches during the tea interval, only to throw up in the pile of bowler's sawdust at the resumption of play. A typical Scorpio.

And there, at number eight, was where the batting strengths finished. Those eight brave men who were able to turn a match (some in the favour of the opposition, it is true).

Alfie Donald was a quiet humourist. Off the field he resembled Sir Jack Hobbs, on the field he resembled nobody at all. Hobbs was fond of pickpocketing for fun, according to the celebrated John Arlott. Donald shared the same hobby, though *his* fun was in not giving the goods back, according to the celebrated *Hackney Gazette*. He shopped by night and bowled by day, off the seam with little turn and even less accuracy, thus swamping the batsmen in vast vats of false security. He was first-change bowler if the day was overcast, or if the faster openers were knackered. Julian followed, and *Pumps Parker* brought up the rear.

Parker wore a box when fielding, bowled with good line and length and, as if it were at all important, he was as gay as Notting Hill carnival. He sported a macho moustache, wore a red lumberjack shirt most of the time, and his car keys jingle-jangled on his trouser belt. His hair was thinning rapidly for a youngster but he would joke about his unusual points with relish. The rest of the players were fond of him, his humour a more than welcome factor during team selection meetings. He was short for a quick bowler but he had all the guts in the world.

And that was the motley crew who left the pavilion to face the gaping mouths once again. They trotted into the outfield, some throwing the ball at Monty, others hurling it high into the sky. A little exercise was needed after the long drive, and about a hundred or so villagers had amassed around the boundary ropes to see the athletes limbering up.

'Like lambs to the slaughter, I believe,' said the vicar.

'Piss off!' exclaimed Kevin Sarling, son of the part-time village policeman, not bothering to turn around to see who was spreading words of doom. By the river, anglers cast hooks at rising dace on the first day of the coarse season, while back in the meadow, one or two young girls cast eyes at the Cockney visitors.

The church bell struck eleven o'clock and the vicar breathed a sigh.

'Dead on,' he muttered gratefully without checking the chimes with anything else. Aubrey Padgett checked the chimes with his watch, as proper as ever.

Aubrey was Little Dow's groundsman and wicket-keeper in the non-playing sense. He was a retired shop-keeper and was about as bright as a ten-watt bulb. Decimalisation had been the downfall of him and his shop, a general store that sold everything in general. He sadly lamented the passing of florin and farthing alike, still charging in old coins long after Queen and country had cancelled their status. His wife had died most suddenly, and Aubrey's life had been at a bit of a loose end. He welcomed the responsibility of groundsman to the cricket team, loved the game he had never mastered and wallowed in the involvement that had come his way. He drove a motor-mower with a seat which rough-cut the square and the outfield, then resorted to a trusty dab of elbow grease to crop the wicket like an army hairdresser. Sometimes Aubrey cleared away the loose cuttings from the outfield, let it rot down then sold it to villagers as compost. Sometimes he didn't. It all depended on the strength of the visitor's batting. Small mounds of green shavings often reduced a cover drive for four to a couple of runs, much to the disbelief and horror of the batsman concerned.

The pavilion resembled the church hall, but had far fewer jumble sales. It was a standing example of green and cream-glossed daubery. Even the outer weather-boarding had been smeared in alternate shades as a multi-coloured gesture by a village carpenter who should have known better. The door groaned for oil and the cobwebbed windows yearned for water. But it was a charming little outbuilding despite its negative points.

Inside was a home-team dressing-room with four coat-hooks and a physiotherapist's table where the cricket bag perched. Between that and the visitor's lounge was a small room with a wash basin and half a bar of soap. Yes, it was certainly verging on the basic, but then all funds from fêtes and village raffles went to the crumbling church, not to the crumbling pavilion. Old photographs of the highest order of fascination hung in the lobby, eternal snaps of nostalgia, depicting the village cricket team from 1947 to the present day. The strange thing was that Joe Robbins appeared in all of them, never looking any older.

The wooden floor bore the gouged out trail of the mobile scoreboard, sadly a scoreboard that had rarely paraded a three-figure grand total. Aubrey repainted the tin numbers at the beginning of summer each year, thankfully preferring black and white to the standardised pavilion colours. He also insisted on manning the apparatus on match days, which may have seemed a little selfish to some but Peter Jackson welcomed the idea — after all, it was one less job for him to sort out.

The home captain thought long and hard about batting order, bowling order and, with the arrival of Creek Cricket Club, law and order. He decided to go for experience to combat keenness of youth. David Baird was left out of the side which was only to be expected, despite a late threatening phone call to Jackson from the boy's irate father. Preference went to Tom Tarry. Baird junior was dismayed; he played well during university term and looked forward to showing off in front of his parents, to say nothing of the rest of the village. His transformation into the highest degree of snobbery was quite astounding. Various minor contributory factors had helped along the way during his first full term at university. He had captured six wickets against the local county side; had outsmarted the local professional football manager during a heated discussion in the university debating chamber; and despite all this, he had still managed to date and spend the night with the female president and her feminist friend from the student's union in a three-for-all one rather drunken weekend after exams. David Baird had everything going for him, ever clear of his eventual destiny. It was hard to take on the role of twelfth man in the boring village cricket team. He was disgusted, his father was embarrassed and his mother patted his head consolingly as she set off to gather in the weekend supplies.

Peter Jackson knew the match would be tough. He had spent the best part of an hour selecting the side. Considering only twelve were available it was hardly a difficult choice, and it was the batting order that was presenting problems. The four previous matches of the season had reaped few runs for Little Dow, so Jackson was hoping for a change in fortune in this game. Aubrey Padgett pondered a little at the tiny slip of paper the captain had given him. He thought he knew the batting order off by heart. This was quite a revolutionary line-up, with an emphasis on youngsters going out there and playing their strokes. The only player to keep his place in the batting order was Joe Baker. Jackson, a moderate man, had thought hard about his side.

'I had thought long and deeply about the batting order. We had failed in our four previous games to turn it on; perhaps the batsmen were playing out of position.

Every cricket side needs a *Joe Baker*, a player who can stay out there seeing off the front-line attack. Joe had undertaken the role with great enthusiasm for the past eight years. He never scored over sixty-five, he never scored under three. He modelled himself on Geoffrey Boycott of Yorkshire and with the demise of the ageing northerner he switched his strokeplay to the straighter bat of Christopher Tavaré of Kent. It was really Hutton dressed up as Lamb, for Baker was not lacking in years, was lacking in flamboyant strokes and stayed at the wicket with the grand intention of reaching double figures. He wasn't the best stroke-player in the side, number one batsmen seldom are, but taking guard alone often took five or six minutes, aggravating the chilly fielders something rotten.

Barnaby Baker opened the batting with the aforementioned Baker J. Although ten years my younger he had become quite a close chum over the last three or four years. We dinner-partied together at least once a month, and with our wives, enjoyed many hours around the bridge table. Barney always bid three clubs when it was actually three no trumps but really that summed up his character. He is cautious, tentative and thoughtful, probably more of a number one than his namesake. We commuted together from the village to Marylebone Station, so had many hours to discuss tactics. He knew exactly what I wanted from him and would give his all to provide it. Barney earned a decent living and dressed smartly, even at the wicket. He wore a light and dark blue striped cap, his shock of blond hair swept back and tucked underneath the unnecessary cloth visor. His cricket bag was adorned by many airline tags, even though he had never taken the contraption abroad. I'm afraid, in that respect, Barnaby was something of a snob; quite possibly it was a means of protest against his lack of inches. I liked him and entrusted him with the task of getting a few runs while Baker J. sent the outfield to sleep.

Geoffrey Baird went in number three because he owned three of the bats and a couple of jock-straps. Hate to say so, but he was worth a few runs too. We lived close to one another but seldom chatted. He was busy organising this and that, and I was busy keeping out of his way. He wore tinted, wire-framed specs as a last-gasp rebellion against approaching middle age (very fetching they were too, even if other wags told him he resembled a welder).

I myself batted number four, my favourite slot in the order, and I fancied myself for a decent score.

John Copeland, though generally as quiet as a church-mouse, was an aggressive player. John, being of the old school was a remarkably well-mannered chap. Do you know he even apologised to bowlers if he smacked a boundary? Dennis Lillee would have hated him. Then came *Philip Trevelyan, Tom Tarry* in his debut match and long-haired *Trevor White* at number eight, a superb bowler who fairly raced at the wicket, his hair flapping behind him like Imran Khan or Sarfraz.

Trevor White was a young right-arm pace bowler of great speed, consistency and energy. He renovated furniture, sold yew replicas and batted left-handed. A keen lad of twenty-seven years, he played for another village on Sunday all-day games, yet lived in neither. His wife Maddy was an unfaithful lass who had fallen in twenty-four-hour love with most male villagers under the age of thirty-five. She had a mind-boggling body, sporting a fine upstanding pair, the likes of which had not been seen since the heady days of Ramadhin and Valentine. Many boundary bushes had swayed to her pleasured sighs at one time or another. Trevor was far too engrossed in the reconstruction of a magnificent but sadly neglected 1863 Chicago harmonium. Renovating the instrument had become a lifelong commitment, carving each new stop with the patience of Trevor Bailey. His hammer and chisel were rested only for bat and pad. He loved his beer to extremes, often generating as much wind as the harmonium he strove to return to working order. That was Trevor, a completely non-aggressive man who bowled like a runaway train rumbling down a steep gradient.

Nicholas O'Connor opened the bowling at the other

end to Trevor. He was medium pace by most standards, yet medium-to-fast by Little Dow's. Maiden overs were his speciality, wickets his hard-earned bonuses and he had played in all the village games during the previous eight years, amassing a grand total of twenty-nine runs. He had been described on various occasions as 'a magnificent bowler and a batsman who promises great things'.

Lord Reginald Smythe lived in twelve acres of privacy beyond the meadow. He was a nice enough old boy, though rarely seen in pub or pavilion. His Range Rover was his own secluded changing area; the leather dashboard housed a rather nifty half-bottle of Cognac and cut-glass tumblers. His wife sat smothered in a tartan blanket, smiling courteously as her husband's teammates wandered by towards the pavilion.

And finally, the ubiquitous, dependable *Joe Robbins*, organiser of village jumble sales, village fêtes, village barn dances and whist drives recurring. Good man at meetings for breaking the oratory ice. Hopeless batsman, never bowled, couldn't field, but his wife made positively exquisite egg and cucumber sandwiches. His mature beer belly was a sight to behold as it flopped over the inadequate circumference of his flannels, and his cricket cap in the rare club colours of black and grey had been supposedly awarded during active service in India. Of course it was nonsense. After all, no man who had witnessed the classic spin of an in-house Indian tussle would know the ball only bounced once before reaching the willow, yet Joe Robbins maintained his style was attributed to his study of the men of the Empire. Such a style enabled the ball to bounce up to five times, at five miles an hour. The ploy was intended to nurture complacency. Joe Robbins had never bowled a solitary soul, but he did coax a catch on the boundary during a village game in 1962.'

Peter Jackson, Winston Waites and the two umpires Parry

Taylor and Lily Grace gathered at the crease at the pavilion end for the toss.

'Looks like holding out, eh?' said Parry.

'Not so sure,' dampened Lily Grace.

'Well, let's get started, shall we?' suggested Peter.

'Yeah, come on, Mr Jackson, let's get the show on the old frog and toad, shall we?' suggested the Creek captain.

'Frog and toad . . . um . . . frog and toad. What on earth is a frog and toad?' asked Lily after a moment's ponder.

'Frog and toad, road, it's cockney rhyming slang. We call the road the frog. Christ knows why. It just makes people look at you,' explained Winston.

Parry Taylor, a kindly, portly gent who lost a leg as a result of a war wound, produced a shining obsolete half-crown from his white coat and presented it to the visitor's captain to spin into the sky. Winston rested the coin on his finger and thumb . . . .

'Heads or tails, Mr Jackson?' the boy asked.

'Good lord, more Cockney rhyming slang? What does heads or tails stand for, young man?' asked the perplexed Lily Grace.

'No, *heads* or *tails*, we're tossing to see who's going to open. OK, Mr Jackson?'

'I'll go for heads.'

Winston tossed the coin. It fell to the grass and four bodies bent down to survey the outcome. It was tails. Creek Cricket Club had won the toss and Winston astutely put the home side in to bat. The two players and two officials strolled back to the pavilion. Both sides seemed delighted with Winston's choice to let Little Dow open the batting.

Blue sky began to show and bearded clouds hobbled through the expanse at pensioner pace. Smoke from leafy bonfires spiralled upwards and the strong smell of apple-wood was deliciously mouth-watering. A pleasure craft passed on the river with its crew sun-bathing on the roof rack as a flotilla of mallard protested at the spectacle. The umpires searched for counting stones, while the two Bakers padded up.

Still the crowd arrived with brightly coloured deckchairs that contrasted with the greyness of the day. Little Dow were all set to get some runs.

'Best of luck, Winston,' enthused Peter Jackson.

'Thanks, Mr Jackson, and the same to you,' replied the office runaround.

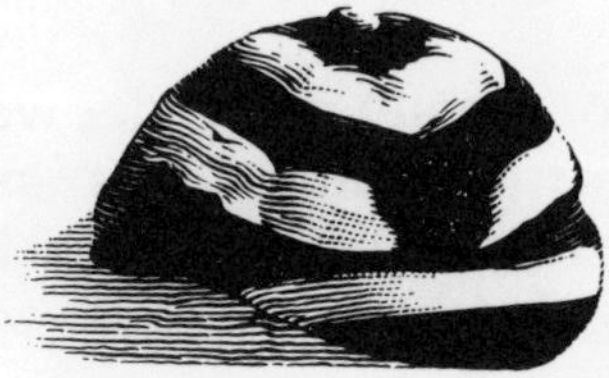

— TWO —

The Morning Session

The morning session finally got under way some eight or so minutes behind schedule. This annoyed Aubrey Padgett who subscribed to the theory that lateness should be punished by a wicket or extra runs — so pernickety was he.

Creek Cricket Club, led by Winston, took to the field to mixed reactions from the Little Dow spectators. Some were shocked to see Slogger Stevenson in his yellow corduroy cricket flannels and Alfie Donald, bobble hat and all, puffing frantically at a roll-up, but others chose to marvel at the awesomely superb physique of Winston and Rudi Waites, Julian Jannik and Vince Clayton, as they charged towards the square like paddocked stallions. No Creek player had ever taken to the field amidst a kindly ripple of applause before. They were absolutely chuffed, and waved to the on-lookers like World Cup football stars.

Up, high into the sky, went the practice ball, down it came into the safe hands of Stevie Whiteman. Up it went again, even higher, and down it came again, this time into the clasped palms of Monty Holt, the wicket-keeper, who had learned the art of custodianship with an old pair of his father's motor-cycle gauntlets. Once again the ball was taken cleanly and tossed lightly to Pumps Parker, who characteristically dropped it. The crowd sighed thankfully.

'I thought they looked rather splendid,' said one deckchair incumbent.

'Know what you mean, Frank,' endorsed his straw-hatted chum, who had witnessed every game at Little Dow since the Coronation.

'Like a snifter?' asked the incumbent opening a hip-flask.

'Not for me, Frank, thanks all the same.'

And so the conversations continued. Some continued to be disgusted at so many whites and colonials in completely the wrong attire, while others were terrified to see the more athletic specimens bounding effortlessly around. Julian Jannik practised a couple of deliveries as the fielding side waited for the appearance of the two openers, causing one sage to change to his reading specs to try to catch the trajectory as Julian turned his arm over.

Back at the pavilion, Aubrey Padgett chewed the end of his pencil and Peter Jackson chewed on his bottom lip. The sun came and went as though short-circuited; Baker B. and Baker J. were more or less set. A wriggle of the bum and the box was in position. Up went the zip and on went the padded gloves that always resembled a cluster of bandaged fingers. Joe rehearsed his favourite strokes into the sullen atmosphere before crossing himself. Despite his non-Catholicism, he thought it was worth a try under the circumstances. Barnaby Baker relieved himself for the second time at the rear of the pavilion. Despite the audible trickle, the allotment tenders ignored his action; they had seen enough for one day, nothing more could stir them.

Montgomery Holt stood resplendent in his claret and blue pads, neither surprised nor perturbed by the various fingers that pointed at him from all sectors of the crowd. He took up his position behind the sticks at the far end of the meadow, the oak tree end. Alfie Donald's stereo headphone gear was met with far less acceptance by the villagers. Their 'tuts' were stage-whisper loud, even though his Japanese apparatus was silent. A few more practice balls homed in on Monty from all directions at great velocity, and the thud of leather on leather resounded around the meadow. He crouched, chuckled and waited for the next torpedo from a team-mate.

Mrs Robbins, Joe's wife of many decades, and her friend Alice from the next cottage edged their way around the perimeter of the playing area at a snail's pace, completely overladen with wicker baskets and carrier bags filled to the brim with country fayre. David Baird, banished to crowd member, trotted to their aid, and Mrs Robbins was only too pleased to accept his gallant offer of help. The entourage picked up a little momentum and as the food was placed in the pavilion the young Baird stole a pickled onion and a scone as severance payment for his trouble.

Winston Waites was arranging his field, sending Slogger to third man, out of harm's way. He was a nifty batsman but a lousy fielder. He hovered in the outfield like a bionic buttercup, his yellow strides more luminous from a distance, reminiscent of a clown in Kerry Packer's low-flying circus. Adjacent to Yellow Legs was Eddie Peters, positioned primarily to cut off the four from the thin edge. By his feet, over the boundary rope, was a Ford car manual and a half-assembled carburettor that hadn't felt the warm glow of carburisation for some time. Between overs or during rainstorms or even when new batsmen made their long trip to the wicket, Eddie would gaze at the malfunctioning object as though it were a rubidious rubic cube, first left, then right, and then a full somersault as the boundary fielder searched for the mechanical fault. The sound of a struck ball would raise his head from the problem, though there was seldom the necessity to do so. Eddie was an opening batsman of integrity, even if he did make the loudish sound of a misfiring car or Derek Randall as the bowler approached, but glorious catches on the boundary were not his forte. He always blamed the sun for his misfielding, even if it were overcast. He never thought of girls, they offered no challenge, what with not coming to pieces.

Eddie and his accessories were well hidden from the batsmen's eyes by Stevie Whiteman who, at short fine leg and forever in black cords, relished the responsibility of fielding for two with startling ability and agility. He retrieved the wickedly snicked ball with arms, legs, rib-cage and even hands. A semi-supremo in the field was Stevie, even though he hardly looked the part. Vulgarities were whispered about him, but his speed was unquestionable and his eye as good as any Little Dow pheasant shooter.

The field was more or less set. Winston nodded his head to approve a minor field adjustment, Donald nodded his in time to a Stevie Wonder cassette. On came the umpires.

'I'll never forget the faces of the Creek players as the two officials strolled so purposefully to the middle. They really thought dear old Lily had been joking when she warned them she was to officiate during the match. Their jaws actually dropped when she marched forward like a civil defence volunteer. Parry Taylor limped as fast as he could but still found great difficulty in keeping up with her ladyship. As well as losing a leg in France during the Second World War, he had managed to lose a Spitfire at the same location but he had been well-decorated despite this carelessness. By all accounts he was a damn fine bowler in his day, and even though he had mastered the artificial limb most admirably, his hours on the cricket pitch were confined to umpiring. His options were minimal since that abortive air raid, but he welcomed the camaraderie of the cricket pitch, the responsibility of the ultimate decision every other over. He hid his abhorrence at the thought of a female umpire. It was hardly cricket, after all. Parry looked around like little boy lost. First at her and then at the attire in the outfield, and even from where I sat by the pavilion I could see the look of puzzled disgust on his face. To him it looked certain to be a bad day for the game he so loved, but in fact he was quite wrong. I wished Baker J. and Baker B. the very best as they set off for the battlefield. The home crowd welcomed the arrival of their trusty openers with a round of warm applause and kind wishes. I was joined by a spectacularly white-clad Tom Tarry and we sat together, all set to assess the skill and accuracy of the opening bowlers.'

Lily Grace checked she had six stones in her right-hand pocket to cancel the balls of the over, then she swept back her hair from her forehead, a little like Marilyn Monroe or Jeff Thomson. She took the fresh, gleaming ball and tossed it to Julian Jannik who rubbed it furiously in the usual place, one inch to the left of obscenity. It was pointless because the ball could not have been cleaner nor shinier. He studied the stitching for no obvious reason and retreated towards the pavilion, measuring his paces as he went. Julian, well used to his captain's wish to act the part, ignored the discussions of field placings in preference to measuring his mighty run-up to the bowler's crease. He placed his white metal disc guide in the ground and chatted to a young, admiring maiden seated a meagre ten feet from the start of his sprint. He undertook agonising squats and arm spins to the delight of the young girl and to the entertainment of the rest of the spectators, who had taken up their positions only a matter of inches from the boundary ropes.

'Give them a chance, lad, they're getting on a bit, you know,' pleaded one.

'Right on, man,' replied Julian in a language never heard before in the musty parish of Little Dow. Julian circulated his long arms downward then skywards. He rubbed the ball once more and the girl's eyes widened.

'Wonder if he needs any help with that,' she murmured to herself, unaware of Julian's fixed gaze on her fixed gaze.

Heads turned as the openers advanced. The unrelated Joe and Barnaby Baker marched in perfect step like two stray infantrymen towards the wicket. An occasional glance towards the heavens assured Barnaby it was still daylight (he had seen Botham do the same thing at the Oval) then he swung his bat in a giant arc (he'd seen the flamboyant Botham do that too). Meanwhile, Joe Baker stopped, buckled at the knees like an old-time village bobby on the beat, and banged his box to ensure it was working then sprinted to catch his chum up. They wished each other the best of luck as they went their separate ways, Barnaby halting by Lily Grace at the pavilion end, and Joe negotiating the extra twenty yards or so on his own. He chewed the end of his glove momentarily, positioned his bat at right-angles to the trimmed grass and called for middle and leg. Madam Grace turned her head, showing an ear, and begged his pardon.

'Middle and leg,' Joe pleaded a little louder. His bat followed the directions of the woman's scarlet fingernails until . . . .

'Middle and leg that is!' she screamed. Baker nodded and prodded until he was quite content.

'Did you hear that old battleaxe?' said Winston to his brother at mid-on.

'Sure did, man, do you know they reckon she was bunged out of the SS for cruelty?' joked Rudi to the delight of all fielders within earshot. Parry Taylor at square-leg umpire position enjoyed the quip too, but disguised his laughter with a tactical cough.

'Hey, man,' roared Monty, 'what about some bleedin' bails then?' Everyone laughed at the oversight, and the crowd joined in the chorus as the word spread, until the whole meadow resounded with a carnival atmosphere. A huge cloud passed overhead, battleship grey, as Joe re-dug the first trench of the day at middle and leg, first with his bat and then with his spiked cricket boots.

'Bowler's name, please,' asked Aubrey Padgett.

'Julian Jannik!' yelled Winston Waites at second slip. Lily Grace's arm came down like a clapperboard, the game was on.

'Right arm over the wicket, six to come.'

Winston shrieked a whistle to his outfield, Eddie dropped his manual while Monty crouched further and further down until only his black head appeared over the claret and blue wicket-keeper's pads. The ground fell silent, the ebb before the flow:

'Good luck, Julian,' said the girl on the boundary, pleased to have heard the bowler's name.

'Thanks, me old darling,' replied Julian. 'See you later, eh?'

'You bet,' confirmed the captured heart.

Every eye fell upon big Julian as he breathed in, staring at the distant batsman. Then the bowler's chest tilted forward, his shoulders broadened and he was on his way, sprinting to the bowler's crease to let fly the first ball of the day. And a handsome delivery it was, too; immense power and accuracy. Julian let out a gasp as the ball shot off the wicket towards Joe Baker, who reared up and played the ball down admirably.

'No ball!' shrieked the lady, just a split second before it reached the defending player.

The delivery caused Baker's fingers to tingle a little, having caught the angry ball too high up the willow. The ball trickled to the non-existent silly mid-on while Julian turned and glared at Lily Grace. What a glare it was, full of superior knowledge of the rules of the fine gentleman's game. Lily was remarkably unimpressed with Julian's predictable display of male chauvinism.

'Unlucky,' comforted the captain.

'Good length, Julian,' called Vince Clayton from mid-wicket.

'Shit,' muttered the bowler.

'Did you see the speed of that thing?' asked one on-looker.

'The speed of what thing,' chuckled another. Little Dow were off the mark, Padgett signalled the acceptance of the call and hastily threw a single on the scoreboard. A glow of great confidence radiated around the pavilion and boundary alike. Julian was fuming as he rubbed the ball even harder, and stamped back to his starting grid. Monty retreated a yard or so further from the stumps, only too aware of his comrade's anger. He had a good idea what was coming down next. One for none was the score.

'Declare while you're winning,' roared a wag.

'Sh . . . sh . . .' ordered the cricket buffs who had already acknowledged that a good battle was in store.

Charlie Turner, the village milkman and pigeon racer, had arrived with his milk bills and was hurriedly handing them out to the customers around the ropes.

'Who's playing?' he asked.

'Some team of Cockneys,' came the reply.

'Cockneys, blooming heck, what are they doing here? I'm off to load up the float,' exclaimed Charlie.

'Don't be silly, lad, these are darn good chappies. Just watch this lad here run up and bowl.'

Turner sat next to his customer, rolling a 'Golden Virginia' as Julian completed the march back to his metal marker. He licked and lit his shag as the bowler turned and then inhaled. Lily heard the ruffling of skin on nylon shirt and the panting of quick breaths beside her left ear (something she hadn't heard for the best part of forty years). Julian sprinted by the official, sideways on, and bowled the next ball short. It dug in the ground like a drill and shot into the air, straight towards the opener's head. The seasoned campaigner ducked and the ball, still rising, was snatched from the air by the agile keeper. Had he missed, it would have penetrated the ozone layer.

'Bloody hell,' groaned Charlie. 'Blow the milk bills, think I'll watch this for a while.' He clapped the excellent delivery, much to the disgust of the older villagers who thought bouncers were only for fiery Australians and headstrong West Indians.

'Time for a bit of spin?' suggested one old-timer.

'Quite so,' replied his pal. 'Ball isn't lifting, damn waste of time if you ask me. Joe can knock those about all day.'

'Quite. Nothing like a spinner, what?'

'Nothing except a double brandy, ha ha.'

'Quite. Ha ha.'

Peter Jackson was impressed with Julian. Two balls were enough to reveal his enormous ability. Julian ran like the great Michael Holding though his legs and hair were longer. It was going to be a tight game all right — Little Dow's experience against the swashbuckling youthfulness of Creek. Jackson wished he was fifteen years younger, then he looked at the young girl admiring Julian and changed his plea to twenty years younger. An ignorant ice-cream salesman, impressed by the gathering, rang his automatic chimes, but to no avail. Only a conscientious angler responded to the bait.

Screwball Pinder touched his toes at silly point, or probably ludicrous point if there were such a placing, and Winston picked the edge of his nose at second slip as the ball returned to the human catapult via three fielders. The crowd increased by four people and one labrador.

Ball number three was on its way. The bowler again trod the measured steps, bypassing the previous day's dog shit, towards the delivery crease. A slower ball, a straight bat, a weak ricochet to Pinder. A misfield and Joe was off the mark. Good cricket! The crowd clapped courteously as the home team's score doubled and the freshly sharpened pencil inscribed the second run into the official Little Dow

Cricket Club scorebook. Jackson commented that Joe was playing sensibly and that Barnaby had decided just to stay out there — a predictable rather than inspired summary after only three balls.

Barnaby took guard of middle stump against Julian. The batsman was fairly efficient off his legs and that particular guard brought him squarer on to the delivery. Only a dreadful mis-hit would find its way into the slips as Barnaby studied the gaps on the on side. As things turned out, Barnaby was fortunate to survive the first ball. He played across the line of the good length ball and the crowd hushed as the solid ball smacked hard against Baker's padded leg. He was plum LBW, well and truly. Julian and Monty leapt into the sky like crazed Jack-in-the-boxes to celebrate the excellent delivery, slips rose too a fraction of a second later. Expectant heads on jigging bodies turned as one to see the lady's one finger of dismissal. The gesture never came and Baker B. was gratefully not out. Julian sustained his appeal, hoping for the guilty conscience to sway the award. He could hardly believe his rotten luck, and in truth it should be said that Baker could hardly believe his either. Julian's war-dance did not cut much ice with Madam Grace and the attacker's head sagged earthward like a wilting flower. He gathered his limp frame together and turned to the offending official.

'Come on, man, what have I gotta do to get this dude?' he begged to the woman who had been miles away at the time, never dreaming that a borderline decision would be necessary so early in the game.

'Extremely adjacent, I would say,' murmured Peter Jackson.

Lily had been thinking of her young niece's trip to Chessington Zoo the previous afternoon, and after the names that had been thrust upon her, she did well to keep her thoughts to herself. Lily Grace would have done well to have gone to the zoo herself, despite the hazardous possibility of a stock-take of the inhabitants occurring.

She chose to ignore the pathetic antics of the muttering Julian until eventually he passed her and the stumps in a far more sombre fashion. She assured him in a loud, crisp whisper, 'I'm not a man, young man, and may I remind you that my decision is final?'

'I don't need reminding,' the bowler assured her.

'Jolly good,' replied Lily Grace.

The slips crouched, legs wide apart, and the outfielders walked a few slow paces forward (with the exception of Eddie Peters who continued to mend his carburettor) and the motion was repeated for two further balls.

'Over!' shrieked the unpopular lady in such a volume that it spilled into the next village and frightened a brace of pheasants from the long grass. Each batsman had sneaked a run and they walked to the centre to discuss the behaviour of the wicket.

Julian grabbed his long-sleeved sweater from Lily Grace and moped back to his boundary retreat. He was not happy.

Baker J.	*not out*	*1*
Baker B.	*not out*	*1*
extras		*1*
TOTAL		*3 without loss*

Winston Waites, conscientious captain, trotted across to meet Julian Jannik as the bowler returned to his field placement. They shared an inter-over chat and judging by the turning of heads and the giggles, it was more about the assembling crumpet than the previous over and the controversial decision. The first six deliveries had been of excellent quality, turning off the seam as they struck the cropped grass, so it seemed crazy to waste time with silly post-mortems when there was so much talent appearing from the riverbank and footpath.

Rudi Waites was due to bowl to Barnaby Baker.

Parry Taylor strolled in from the square-leg umpire position, his body lifting as his artificial left leg bent at its artificial knee-cap. He juggled with the six stones in his white decorator's coat as his portly frame towered over the undisturbed stumps. He raised his arm to ensure the eager Rudi didn't bowl while Barney was surveying the battlefield. The blue touchpaper was lit and Rudi held the firework in an ungloved hand. Brother Winston sprinted back to the slips having instigated a few minor adjustments in the field and Baker took guard for the second time. The peak of his old boy's cap was pulled down firmly to his eyebrows, Geoffrey Boycott fashion, and with his backside protruding adjacent to the bails he resembled a constipated mallard.

Big Rudi sprinted towards the game batsman, the ball changing hands en route. The sheer ferocity of the lad brought gasps of disbelief from the crowd. Barnaby had intended a stroke but the delivery quite simply hadn't given him the time to think of one. There was a split-second silence as Baker played into mid air and then a familiar crack of leather on wood resounded around the peaceful meadow. Baker B. was clean bowled. The fielders raced in to congratulate their flying torpedo. The bemused but appreciative crowd looked on applauding, as the team slapped hands in the Jamaican mode to celebrate the drawing of the first blood.

Barnaby Baker, feeling dejected and hideous, walked back to the rejected and hideous pavilion, his mallard beak bowed low towards the soil, as though he were searching for consolation worms.

'Damn good ball that, Barney old boy,' called a local.

'Just your luck to get that one,' consoled another.

'How's the wicket?' asked Joe Robbins, looking positively absurd in mottled, bottled glasses that needed hawk-like eyes to see through. Barnaby didn't take in a single remark, didn't answer a single query, so cross was he.

'Where were you? What happened?' he pleaded to himself, disgusted at his feeble innings and low score. His head never rose until he had crossed the boundary ropes, and even then it was eyes full ahead as he chose to ignore Geoffrey Baird, the in-going batsman. Not a solitary word, such was the Little Dow tradition. Baird approached the wicket slowly, with caution, while Alfie Donald changed the side of his Stevie Wonder cassette, turning down the volume, fancying his chances of taking a splendid boundary catch. Baird looked around at the field that was offered him. He saw few gaps, for Winston and Rudi were far too astute to allow that sort of thing. No, Baird would have to earn his runs. It was approaching eleven-thirty as he prodded at the popping crease with a nagging, nervous regularity. Jackson looked pensive beneath his blue and yellow-hooped school cricket cap which made his head resemble a piece of mature Stilton.

Rudi advanced for the second time, faster than most county sprinters, neater than any county middle-distance runner. But it was a loose ball, a full toss that hurtled towards Baird's thigh pad before being gratefully deflected away towards the mid-wicket boundary for four runs. A splendid shot which Eddie Peters thought twice about retrieving, even though he had very little choice. The relieved spectators applauded the fine shot with the rich clanging of chilly hands it so rightly deserved. Geoffrey touched his cap like the other Geoffrey of Yorkshire and England, and absolutely nothing was said by the fielders.

Twelve more deliveries, six apiece from Jannik and Waites, and that fine stroke remained the solitary boundary, even though a few well-taken singles were called by both batsmen, who were responding well to the accurate seam attack. A good return throw at the boundary from the arm of Vince Clayton had almost knocked Lily Grace's head off. Taking her gently by the arm Winston Waites, forever the gentleman, enquired about her well being, though his team-mates maintained an eloquent silence.

A couple of hundred tame raindrops had landed on the outfield with not so much as a splash, but the fielders complained more about Clayton's inaccurate throw than they did at the drops of rain. The weather was holding; the clouds looked aloof rather than menacing as they raced through the blue yonder, and Geoffrey Baird raised the collar of his neat shirt as he had seen them do on Test highlights on TV.

Baird was a tall man, well over six foot. Many said he spent far too much time in his greenhouse, and his stalking height more than verified the rumour. His tinted glasses hid his eyes like welder's goggles and his hair, though thinning around the apex, was lengthy around the ear lobes. He was forty-five pushing twenty and loudly boasted the virtues of John Coltrane and J.J. Johnson to people who had never heard of them. He chose not even to smile at the bombardment of Lily Grace, though he was as surprised as the next man that not a solitary man had the decency to warn her of the dangerous proximity of Clayton's return throw. Lily was more than a little determined. There would not be the faintest possibility of an LBW decision in this innings . . . not any more.

Aubrey Padgett placed the final dot of the over in the official scorebook with pedantic care and raced to grab the drinks tray from the half-paced Mrs Robbins. He had probably picked Sir's chalk off the floor when he was a schoolboy, though his creased looks and stoop were proof of the many years that had passed since such halcyon days. Mrs Robbins, the robbed Mrs Robbins, stormed back to the pavilion releasing blue adjectives towards the grey sky. The artificial luminosity of the orange squash radiated from the square to the folk behind the boundary ropes like a vitaminic strobe light. Pumps Parker belched loudly and unforgivably as he replaced the empty glass on Aubrey's tray, and Lily glared into his neck with such penetration he turned around and apologised. Alfie Donald appreciated the incident and giggled as they crouched for the next delivery. Clayton called him a stupid iron, a most uncalled-for taunt.

The next ball ripped into the cropped strip. It was a beautiful delivery by young Jannik, the ball turning and lifting. It shot off the dampened wicket and Joe Baker lifted a straight bat to the fearsome thing, but the ball rose too high, ricocheting into the safe hands of the offended Alfie Donald at silly point.

'Owzat,' screamed most, and up went the arms of the jubilant fielders simultaneously with the index finger of the umpire. Joe Baker was, not for the first time or last time in his part-time career, dismissed cheaply. The fielding side was delighted, the crowd's disappointment was hidden beneath the warm, generous applause it afforded the bowler and catcher. Donald had never been applauded before so he felt ten feet tall as he ran to his team-mate, and as they hugged in celebration the close fielder planted a smacker of a kiss on the cheek of the startled Clayton.

'What did you call me?' asked Alfie Donald with a threatening clenched fist, then the two chums slapped hands in the traditional way and collapsed on to the carefully mown grass in delirious laughter. The audience clapped in the unfortunate Baker J. with consolatory calm. Julian Jannik was chuffed with a wicket under his belt, and swaggered to the mid-wicket boundary to confirm a date with the young girl who had patiently sat awaiting his first approach. She would be well rewarded, for both were immensely impressed with each other.

Peter Jackson had all but selected his favourite bat at the dismissal of Baker J., and as he foraged through the club kit-bag Winston Waites, office junior and opposing skipper, crossed the ropes and bounded towards him.

'Everything all right, Mr Jackson?' asked the lad.

'Oh . . . er . . . er . . . yes thanks, Winston old pal, what about your chaps? Are they enjoying themselves out there?' he queried.

'Oh, I should say so, man. Hey what d'you think of Julian Jannik's bowling. Pretty hot ain't it?' giggled the wicked boy.

'I should say so, bloody good bowler that lad, what about taking him off? Just for your good old Mr Jackson?' Jackson suggested.

'Take him off? Take him off?' said Waites very loudly, causing pipe puffers to cease puffing and sandwich nibblers to cease nibbling. 'You gotta be joking. Julian Jannik can bowl all day if he wants to, and most of the next day too. It wouldn't surprise me at all if at the end of the innings he went and gave that lady umpire one just for the sheer hell of it, man,' Winston roared, in such appreciation of his own humour that Peter Jackson was embarrassed, though he still managed to offer his office junior a diluted smile.

> 'You could have knocked me down with a feather when young Waites came out with that comment. My face turned as red as a match ball. That evening I thought of Julian Jannik giving Lily Grace one and I must confess I collapsed at the very thought, but at the time I hardly knew where to put my face. I was only too pleased that I was the in-going batsman. I turned away from the old-fashioned looks of the upstanding members of the village and strolled purposefully towards the stumps. The village church struck mid-day and by the time I was at the wicket taking my guard it was afternoon.'

'Disgusting behaviour,' complained Nancy Cartwright to her deck-chaired companion Polly Townes.

'Quite so, Nancy. What will he give her one *of*?'

'Oh never mind, Mrs Townes, never mind dear, so long as you found it disgusting it's all right.'

'I did, Nancy, I did. It's the younger generation, you know. If my Tom were alive he would have had a heart attack,' she assured her companion.

'Just as well he didn't bother to come back from the grave to see this then, my dear, it would have been a bit of a waste of time I feel, God bless him.'

'Yes, God bless you, Tom,' said Polly Townes. 'You keep out of harm's way, dear. It's getting too smutty down here. Now listen, Nancy, I'm not one to be prejudiced, not me. I'm not blaming the lad for being black. He could be yellow with bright blue spots for all I care. No there's no prejudice, I just don't like young people. They've got nothing to live for like they did in our day you know.'

'Quite true, quite true. Oh look, that nice Mr Jackson's going in to play now. He is such a very polite young man,' enthused Nancy Cartwright.

Baker J.	*ct Donald*	*b Jannik*	*16*
Baker B.		*b Waites R.*	*1*
Baird	*not out*		*22*
Jackson	*not out*		*0*
extras			*4*
TOTAL			*43 for 2 wickets*

Jackson took centre stump guard and prodded the virgin area of the popping crease an inch or so distant from Joe Baker's middle and leg trench. He surveyed the field placings, noticing nothing in particular, then settled, crouching, for Julian's arrival at the bowling crease. The amiable villager saw off the over before prodding and lightly stepping his way towards the centre of the wicket for a quick chat with Geoffrey Baird. Even in the pub their conversations were brief, to say the least. At the wicket, fewer words could hardly have been said.

'All right?'

'Yep. You?'

'It's turning.'

'Yep.'

And then the pair strolled back to their rightful positions. It was a cricketing ritual the pair hated. Baird was resentful on his son's behalf that he had not been included, but Jackson couldn't give a damn.

Rudi Waites polished one side of the ball furiously on his flannels, his determination evident in the tautness of every muscle. What had started out as a nice trip into the Buckinghamshire countryside was developing into an important fixture that neither side wanted to lose. Little Dow had reputations at stake, Creek had reputations to seal with certain villagers. It wasn't a league match but neither was it a friendly.

Rudi had gained the fine opening figures of one for eleven with two maidens to his credit. This was the last over of his first stint, and he was to be replaced by the far slower but arguably more accurate Alfie Donald (well, Donald argued that he was, anyway). Jackson played a couple of balls masterfully, with a couple of others he was blessed with a little luck, and at the end of the over his wicket was still intact and he had somehow forced a single off the last ball via his back pad. He was off the mark. Rudi Waites collected his sweater and two gold chains from the umpire and Baird decided not to meet his skipper halfway on this particular occasion. Jackson kept strike and Baird kept his distance.

Sure-footed Winston Waites pointed hither and thither complacently as he ordered the players to their positions. Donald was to bowl. The pair discussed field placings and a few female members of the crowd at the oak-tree end. Parry Taylor limped from his square-leg umpiring position to join them but said nothing, preferring to whistle and shuffle his counting stones. Lily Grace adjusted her dress as she shot off towards an adjacent vantage point. Her lips were bright red, as though that rascal Rudi had polished the ball on them; her cheeks too were tinged rouge like his flannels and her permed hair, although nothing whatsoever like *his* permed mop, sat rigid on her head like a concrete bird's nest.

Alfie Donald was the archetypal shorty, his little white legs taking far more steps than those of his black friends to reach the bowling crease. He was the team celebrity and found no difficulty in differentiating between good solid mates like Winston, Rudi and Vince Clayton, and the 'easy blag' at the cricket club Friday-night disco. His flannels were a size too generous, his shirt a shade too dark, his hair was a length too untidy and his humour was usually one obscene gag too much. Yet this game and the travelling beforehand had found the new bowler in a sombre mood. The Little Dow crowd thought him a quiet lad who said very little. The Creek mob knew better. The blond-haired shorty was out of salts, there was no doubt about it. He didn't like the surroundings, which had made him feel uncomfortable. He was used to groups of noisy kids screaming insults from the boundary ropes, he was used to dogs making whoopee at short extra cover. None of this toffee-nosed middle class stuff, it wasn't for him.

Douglas R. Jardine was the same, of course, on his first trip to the Land of the Convicts in the 1928–29 season. He hated Australians in general and Australia in particular, even though he had met merely a handful of his colonial counterparts (even stranger that Jardine himself, although of Scottish parentage, was born in India). He did not offer his hand across the sea and was master of the supercilious stare.

Alfie Donald played a similar part and most unfair it was, for the Little Dowers had shown tremendously kind hospitality to the merry entourage despite the sheer novelty of it all. Donald was probably well aware of all that; it was simply that it was an alien world, heard-of but hitherto unwitnessed. He felt vulnerable without his East End backdrop of towering flats and giant factory chimneys where a guy could easily lose himself within the anonymity of the setting. This was different, and despite the splendid catch he had held at silly point he felt inferior.

Donald pulled his buttermilk slipover over his unkempt mop and tossed it to Parry Taylor, who stuffed it under his arm. Donald nodded and Winston pointed. Some players moved six or seven feet, Julian returned to the playing area and once more Parry Taylor's arm came down like a barrier at the frontier. The thickening, gossiping throngs fell silent as the short lad hurtled his first ball to the waiting Peter Jackson. A well-flighted delivery. For a second or two it hung in the air, then it was played solidly back to Donald with a straight bat. Eyes meet eyes . . . batsman gently smashes ant on the head as it dares to cross the cropped wicket on its way home . . . the same again and then cubed. Another fine maiden over, a commendable first six deliveries from Alfie Donald.

Jackson had this habit of taking on the role of radio commentator while he was at the crease, claiming it held his concentration while the fielding side flung a few jokes around the outfield. He leaned on his bat having successfully negotiated Donald's first over, and glanced at Aubrey Padgett's scoreboard and Lily Grace's wristwatch. More runs were needed in the next few overs. Creek Cricket Club certainly had the upper hand.

> '. . . And it's the athletic Julian Jannik from the pavilion end, running in to Geoffrey Baird who's looking quite comfortable on a couple of dozen smartly taken runs. And that's a bad ball, pitched far too near Baird's legs, and the experienced batsman fairly cracks that on the half-volley through the covers for four more runs. Screwball Pinder retrieves from the decaying daffodil stems near the river as the score moves along quite nicely to 48 for the loss of two wickets, and can I have another piece of cake please, Trevor.'

Peter Jackson smiled at his own particular brand of humour and smiled too at Baird's splendid shot as Lily signalled to the scorer.

'. . . The appreciative crowd applaud the stroke and Baird looks good. No, on second thoughts he looks a total pain in the arse, nose in the air like some poncey, strutting peacock. Shame he's so bloody good. Fred?'

'Well, if I were bowling to a man of such obvious class and ability I'd merely concentrate on line and length. I just don't know what's going off out there.'

Jackson dropped the Yorkshire accent, adjusted his box and sprinted a quick couple of runs, spitting lightly towards mid-on. He thoroughly enjoyed narrating the critical appraisal of the opposition, telling the listeners all over the country and listeners to World Service who had just joined him of the weaknesses of the foe. Nobody heard his expert analyses but he would have been forgiven for living out his fantasy. He needed the pretence of a John Arlott existence. He tired easily of the Law Society paragraphs that spurted from his lips during the working day; in private life such garrulous prose was a waste of time to those not of the Bar. Back at the Plough the report of the Crown *v* Fred Bloggs 1982 would have gone down like a French kiss at a family reunion. His impressions were far more tolerable, even if they were hopeless, but weekends were family or fairy tale, a time when Jackson lost ten or fifteen years. His wife understood, even if his children hadn't noticed. End of the over and a change of bowling. Creek's tactics were to keep Julian Jannik at the pavilion end for a while whilst alternating the attack at the oak-tree end, and so not permit the batsmen to settle down to one particular style. Winston replaced brother Rudi, allowing the latter to nip off for a quick pee beyond third man.

'Owzat!' screamed Monty in a style that would have qualified him for an Equity card, his arm raised in victorious salute, his legs dancing like a crazed exhibitionist at a disco. Parry was absolutely correct with the official decision, for not only was Jackson playing well forward, but it was also bat and pad. The LBW appeal did not stand.

'Not out!' declared Parry Taylor.

'Thank God for that,' whispered the batsman.

'Shit,' mumbled the curbed wicket-keeper.

Jackson's heart kicked an extra shot of adrenalin through the appropriate channels as he settled himself for the next ball. He screwed up his eyes and focused on the raised arm of Winston Waites as it swung in mid air before releasing the ball towards him. Jackson stepped forward one pace and swung his bat like the legendary Jessop. There was a hard crack of wood and the ball screamed within a foot or so of the scoreboard. Various members of the crowd yelled the value of the shot (six runs) and even the respectful fielders applauded the man's gigantic hit over mid-off. It was the first six of the match. Lily at the square-leg umpiring position raised her arms as a matter of course, showing off her pretty, frilly, pink petticoat hem in the process. The batsman was delighted with the long hop, checking his bat for any after-effects. Winston wasn't so ecstatic.

'There was no-one more surprised than me when that ball flew into orbit. I hadn't hit a six for over two seasons, though it should be noted I broke two fingers trying to repair a dickey lawn-mower, and also played a lot of tennis the year before last. Young Waites was none too happy. I waited patiently as he lengthened his run, glancing regularly at yours truly with vengeful eyes. I wasn't that bothered. After all the six was rather glorious. Even Baird had been reluctantly impressed, so a dismissal next ball would hardly have been disaster for me. I tried to keep my cool, staring at the extra clouds that had arrived overhead, a little whiter than those of the morning procession but most unwelcome all the same. The umpire's arm fell to his side and Winston leaned forward. I looked down and placed my bat on the popping crease, tapping the turf lightly in time with the lad's steps. It was totally silent, I felt naked and absurd. The wicket-keeper groaned as he crouched behind the stumps.'

Winston Waites tore in with all the venom and rage he could muster. He was not an aggressive sort of boy, despite his huge black frame, but he pretended well. His feet stamped hard on the outfield as he strode in at full pace in a slightly curved run-up. The furious paceman dug the delivery into the wicket on a ridiculously short length. The scarlet blur of a cricket ball lifted dangerously, homing in on Jackson's head. Lower-order batsmen by the pavilion and closer fielders gasped as the ball raced towards the wicket. Jackson swerved around, dipped his right shoulder and looked set to allow the wicked delivery to pass safely through to Monty behind the stumps. Temptation was too much, he played outside the off stump, prodding his bat as high as his shoulder. It was a pathetic stroke and the ball shot into the air. Screwball Pinder's hands were free, because his cigarette was in his mouth at the time, and the delinquent took an easy catch to dismiss Little Dow's captain. Jackson raised his head to the heavens, seeing nothing that he hadn't seen a few minutes beforehand. Winston was joined by brother Rudi and Pumps Parker and they pranced around as though participating in some tribal war dance. The dismissed batsman tucked his bat under his arm, removed one padded glove and set off in the general direction of the pavilion. He exchanged a few words with the bowler as they crossed paths but few knew exactly how Jackson felt.

'I was darned well depressed. Utterly pissed off as a matter of fact. How would you feel if you were dismissed by your office boy?'

'Well bowled, Winston old pal.'
'Well batted, Mr Jackson sir, good six that.'
'Yes, must have been delighted to see the back of me!'
The members of the mutual appreciation society went

their separate ways, Winston to the puffing Pinder who had surprisingly held the catch, Jackson off to the ropes to the customary niceties from the on-lookers by the green and cream pavilion. Winston had bowled wisely and had slain his giant. Well played Winston Waites.

John Copeland was already halfway towards the crease as the dismissed Peter Jackson reached into his flannels for his redundant protective box. He handed the contraption to Philip Trevelyan, the next chap in, who subsequently scampered off to the washroom in the pavilion, pretending to wash his face and hands, pulling himself together for his ensuing knock, but in truth he doubted the cleanliness of Jackson's privates. Jackson squatted next to the scorer, lit his pipe and pondered on what might have been. He was disappointed but not suicidal; Copeland was always good for a few runs. There was still an hour before lunch as Peter was joined by Lord Reginald Smythe. The pair glanced at the scorebook:

Baker J.	*ct Donald*	*b Jannik*	*16*
Baker B.		*b Waites R.*	*1*
Baird	*not out*		*26*
Jackson	*ct Pinder*	*b Waites W.*	*7*
Copeland	*not out*		*0*
extras			*5*
TOTAL			*55 for 3 wickets*

Jackson was pleased to learn that his splendid six had brought up the fifty, though he was blissfully ignorant that some of the loud appreciation could have been for that landmark, as opposed to his shot.

Many of the Creek members hadn't really begun the game in the best of spirits. Some ridiculed the pot-bellied middle-class opposition, others were too hung over to really have much idea of what was going on. Screwball set tongues a-wagging with his first comment by the pavilion steps.

'Hey, Stevie, have you ever been so drunk you've gone

to kiss a bird on the lips, missed, and kissed her on the navel?' he asked loudly.

'Blimey, I've been drunker than that,' replied the impish Stevie.

A couple of overs had been played indifferently, but Geoffrey Baird looked set for a fine innings and the Creek side resented the idea of humiliation by an older side. They had the bit between their teeth, headaches were put to the back of their heads and even the arrival of the highly Jewish-looking John Copeland barely stirred the humour buds of the outfielders.

Rudi asked Vince Clayton if he had heard of the Jew who said that if God had wanted him to fly he would have given him a ticket, but Clayton didn't understand the joke, nor was he keen to show good humour at a time when good fielding was far more important. He was apprehensive of the score that Baird was accumulating. Rudi Waites was brought back at the far end to contain the free-scoring batsman, and although he managed to force John Copeland to snick the ball for a caught behind, Geoffrey Baird, the troublemaker and most vital scalp, still remained at the crease — on occasions as stubborn as Tavaré, then opening up in true Colin Milburn spirit.

Baird and Trevelyan lived in the same cluster of thatched houses, but heavy business commitments insured the two never met, allowing them to have conversations only between the stumps or at local council meetings. Philip Trevelyan was a quiet chap in his early forties who had been in the village over five years, yet still very few of his neighbours actually knew what he did for an honest crust. Youngsters thought he was a Russian spy, others who were older and should have known better thought he was an Argentinian spy. In truth he was a naturally quiet man who kept himself to himself and worked in the accounts office of a yacht chandlers' business in London's Devonshire Row, just down the cobbled road from Jackson and Baker B. He preferred to travel alone each morning, absorbed in a different book every other day. He loved cricket almost as much as he loved his wife Jenny, a beautiful woman who, at that moment, sat shivering a little next to the towpath adjacent to the trees. Philip was a good-looking man who had light brown hair with occasional streaks of grey to confirm the passing years, and a slightly built frame on feet that had knocked in a few good goals in their day. But as far as football was concerned, these days he couldn't hit a good ball if he stood on a rake, and football's loss was Little Dow Cricket Club's gain. He was a conscientious member who took charge of subscriptions, match fees and refreshment reimbursements. His boyish parting was just to the left of the top of his head, and his guard was just to the left of middle stump.

At twenty-two minutes past one Baird cut a beautiful square drive for four and his fifty was up. The hundred or so spectators stood in appreciation and the batsman raised his bat in acknowledgement, walloping himself on the bridge of his nose in the process. The blow made his eyes water and the Creek boys thought he had been overcome with emotion. Pumps Parker called him a 'squirmey little ginger' which made Alfie Donald raise his eyebrows. There followed a few minutes of survival batting before lunch, but Trevelyan got off the mark with a blistering attempt at a six that trickled past second slip for a single. The inclement weather was a worrying factor, and a newsflash concerning the death of a motor-racing champion blared out from a transistor radio.

'Serves 'im darned right if you ask me,' declared Tom Lindell, an overweight walking beer barrel from Lindell's Farm. He was a fine one to talk, swinging his tractor around the blind bends of Little Dow and surrounding areas with complete disregard for oncoming traffic. 'Call that a sport? I'd rather blast the 'ead off a pheasant anyday.'

Lily Grace lifted off the bails at the pavilion end. Lunch. And well timed it was too, for the breeze of the river was stiffening a little and a few more spots of rain dropped in from above. Baird and Trevelyan marched pavilion-bound in complete formation, right left, right left, with Geoffrey Baird, the odiously fine village cricketer, acknowledging the applause with polite if supercilious nods. Creek's fielders followed to a richly-deserved round of clapping for good fielding and fine sportsmanship. Eddie jostled with his aluminium, mechanical rubic cube as he brought up the rear and Julian shot off to the long grass with his new-found friend. Lunch was to be served in the grand lounge of the Plough Hotel, with all expenses met by the home side's club funds, Jackson having explained the cash-flow problems of most of the opposition.

Curious eyes glanced at Aubrey Padgett's neat handwriting in the scorebook as both sides mingled before setting off down the towpath to Little Dow's sole macadamised strip that was the main road. It made interesting reading.

Baker J.	*ct Donald*	*b Jannik*	*16*
Baker B.		*b Waites R.*	*1*
Baird	*not out*		*51*
Jackson	*ct Pinder*	*b Waites W.*	*7*
Copeland	*ct Holt*	*b Waites R.*	*2*
Trevelyan	*not out*		*2*
extras			*6*
TOTAL			*85 for 4 wickets*

Baird explained to a young autograph hunter that he preferred hitting boundaries to running for singles and twos as he unpadded and went off to wash his hands for lunch. It had been a magnificent, undefeated knock, and he looked good for a few more after eats. What a shame he was such an objectionable fellow. The opposition spoke highly of his ability as they left the outfield, so it was rather a pity that his own side thought he was an arrogant bore. Why was he so good at everything? The question flashed from fielder to fan as the entourage besieged the public house.

Mrs Setters and Martha, a temporary barmaid-cum-domestic charlady, set out bowls of game soup in lines along the dozen or so tables that filled the lounge area. She had borrowed the recipe and some spoons from the White Swan, a local hostelry of extortionate tariff that preferred to appeal to the visitor on a country trip rather than a skint local. Mounds of French bread appeared, heaped into wicker baskets.

The teams wandered in at a leisurely pace, laughing loudly at banal mid-day comments, the way that studious part-time cricketers seem to. Mentions of straight bats, true wickets, and perfect atmospheric conditions for flight in the air, abounded from all directions. Baird's fifty runs were anatomised and praised as peckish players pecked at the *hors d'oeuvres*.

Winston and Vince Clayton enquired about the juke-box and fruit machine, raising eyebrows of the lunchtime gathering of the cribbage school, an elite collection of old sages who required fifty or so years and an ability to count to thirty-one to allow membership. Fifteen-two, fifteen-four was a far more familiar sound at that particular watering hole than the rhythmic poundings of Bob Marley and the Wailers on vinyl.

Eddie Peters had made the acquaintance of a cobwebbed villager who had bought a model-T Ford brand new. They sat deep in conversation with moving arms enacting piston movements and nodding heads confirming agreement or understanding. The disbelieving boundary fielder dribbled with ecstasy as the old man told his tale, and upon realisation that the mint condition beast was garaged a meagre stone's throw from their wooden bench, he yelled with delight — a born-again car mechanic. Even so, above his wondrous yelps came the authoritative scream of rank — fifteen-six, two for a pair and one for his knob.

Such counting systems meant little to the visiting side, and indeed their visit meant even less to the crib school. Eddie helped his new pal to his feet, handed him his flat cap and cane and they left the bar as keen as youngsters netting at Lord's.

Molly Martin anticipated great things too — in the privacy of her parent's gingerbread cottage beneath the vast shoulder-blades of one Julian Jannik. It had all begun with the bowler's innocent squats on the boundary and had progressed to his attempting double top in the long grass by the river. This was much to the annoyance of the ice-cream-licking angler who, on the first day of the coarse season, was trying to tempt a fine chub with a cherry and was experiencing far less co-operation than Julian. He continued his dapping long after Julian and Molly were stretched out on her mother and father's bed. Thank heavens her parents enjoyed the fresh air of a cricket match on the meadow; if not, such delight would never have been experienced by these highly indulgent couple of modern romantics. Tongue wrestled searchingly with tongue as French kiss followed French kiss. Julian seemed to overheat. Eddie Peters' chum had complained of a leaky radiator, Julian had the same sort of problem. He unbuttoned his shirt, then helped Molly with a hand steeped in the East End tradition of undressing unsuspecting madams in the hope of a quick fondle. Julian remembered the cricket match, wondered how long the lunch interval would last, then disregarded the whole sporting occasion as Molly gently rubbed him around the red dye on his cricket flannels.

'Oh, sod it!' Julian whispered to himself.

'Do you have a girlfriend back in London?' Molly enquired, fiddling about with his ears.

'Sort of, I s'pose, but she's got the old hump with me she has.'

'Why's that?' asked Molly nosily.

'Well . . . um . . . she asked me why I never told her I loved her while I was making love.'

'And what did you say to her?'

'Because you're never there!'

Julian shrieked with laughter, Molly screamed her approval and the pair were sharing the most intimate of poses before you could say Srinivasraghavan Venkatarghavan of Tamil Nadu.

Lily Grace passed the lunch interval in the officials' area, a narrow lobby between the home side's dressing-room and the one-basin washroom. In a cracked mirror she peered at her face in search of cracked make-up. Under construction went her face, first with cream and then with a black wedge of mascara around her slightly sagging eyes. Beneath her tweed hat her hair was as grey as a winter's day thunderstorm, yet as dry as a midsummer stream. She had wished for many years to play the game herself but cricket at village level was a sport for the husbands, so umpiring was her substitute, the only involvement allowed by the ancient rules of gentlemen.

Good umpires were hard to come by, usually resulting in the official being a member of the batting side who had already proven the inability to master his rules of LBW or decent bowling by sacrificing his wicket earlier on in the proceedings. A white decorator's coat and six stones, they were the only *real* qualifications for an umpire, but at least at Little Dow the umpires were conscientious folk, not reincarnated batsmen, and it must be said that Parry Taylor was more than proficient in compensating for Lily's occasionally wayward decision. He kept the game going in good spirits, recorded every over in his notepad, and studied every run for a short call or a run out. Parry Taylor was much admired, and his hunched frame and jovial portly face were always welcomed at grounds throughout Buckinghamshire. Compliments even flowed from the Creek players, though that was partly due to exasperation brought on by his female counterpart. They respected Parry Taylor's knowledge of the game and the tasteless Clayton compared him to Stevie Whiteman, saying they both had the ability to become legless.

Parry would have accepted the pun in good humour had he too slipped down to the Plough Hotel for lunch, but that wasn't the war veteran's style. He usually sat alone with his thoughts in the umpire's enclosure, but the pungent waft of sweet lavender talcum powder and other nostril-twitching accessories had driven him to the solitude of the saloon bar of the White Swan. However Parry, always the perfect gent, would never complain, choosing to refer to Lily Grace as a fine female specimen (and indeed she was, with a sense of humour as vast as her massive thighs).

Parry had peeped his head around the creaking door as Lily emulsioned her lips with her stick of scarlet underseal, pressing them together to cement the layer. Her head turned first to the left and then to the right as she searched her reflection for flaws in her make-up, yet she still failed to spot Parry observing her. Lily was pushing up her hair into a bun, forcing body into the lifeless strands, as Parry slipped away across the outfield to the sanctuary of Little Dow's alternative alcoholic hostel. The beer was a few pence dearer, the idle bar talk was dreadfully-awfully, splattered with comments about pheasant shooting and Young Conservative banter, but Parry never cared — the privacy was worth all that.

The White Swan stood at the other end of the village to the Plough Hotel, a hundred yards or so beyond third man, and it attracted a completely different type of drinker, he that would never object to the few extra pennies on the short measures. A pub well suited for a drink in the country and a hosteller well suited to his clientele, and ignored by most of the villagers. For some strange reason his saloon bar walls were bedecked with overposed shots of past village cricket sides. The landlord had never seen a single game, but he did wonder what all the din was coming from the meadow every other Saturday or Sunday afternoon during the summer months.

The umpire raised his glass of ale, winking at its clearness, then poured it slowly down his gullet with the skill and assurance of a seasoned drinker. The froth bubbled around his top lip like a sergeant-major's moustache until the thirsty man sucked in the stray hops. It was a welcome sup, for a few hours at the stumps was thirsty work.

Parry Taylor placed the empty glass on the end of the bar, purchased a box of matches and rolled his tongue around moist lips as he headed back towards the meadow. The whistling birds noticed nothing as they flew and swooped overhead in search of nesting places beneath the thatched roofing. He lit his pipe and puffed gently, taking in both the smoke and the beauty of life, so grateful to still be part of it all, despite the absent limb. A most enviable fellow was Parry Taylor.

Lily Grace also rolled her tongue around her lips. She took a final glance at the musty mirror and adjusted her suspenders in haphazard fashion before walking into the glare of daylight. She received no applause for her re-entry like the umpires of a Test match, for she was merely a human signal to conclude the lunch interval. Chewing folk peered at her premature arrival, because scotch eggs were barely nibbled beyond the breadcrumbs and coleslaw was still heaped on the side of the paper picnic plates. On top of that, the players were still laughing and joking at the Plough, with the East End lads particularly enjoying the real ale. She stroked the post mistress's labrador affectionately, only too aware that the bitch was the only viewer of the morning session who had sat through it all without commenting on her umpiring. The dog had left a token of appreciation at deep mid-wicket but Lily couldn't care less as the placid beast filled her wrinkled, offered hand with canine saliva.

Julian Jannik reached across Molly's admirable features to the bedside cabinet, his big bleary eyes searching for his discarded wristwatch. It had to be approaching the end of the lunch period, and Julian observed the recall to duty. Molly never stirred, laying sound asleep at his side, her lips gently twitching like the cat that had the cream.

'Christ, she doesn't half look tasty with her old bonce on the weeping willow like that,' the knackered medium pacer thought to himself. He hoisted his cricket flannels from around his ankles to their original length of the day. Molly moved slightly as he buttoned up his shirt, but never awoke. He ignored the perspiration stains and fragrance of two sports in one day as he groomed his hair with his fingers. There was no necessity to leave a note of thanks, for she knew where her lover would be when she awoke. Molly would follow to the meadow whenever her energy allowed. Julian whistled nothing in particular as he left the little cottage by the back garden door. A neighbour's curtain fluttered back into position but Julian didn't give a hang. He had never been in a thatched cottage before, but that was hardly the innocent thought on his mind as he closed the gate behind him and headed for the anti-climatic glamour of second-class cricket. 'Blimey, I'm cream crackered and starving hungry,' thought the ungrateful sportsman as he strolled purposefully down to the towpath. 'I reckon my belly thinks my throat's been bleedin' cut,' he went on.

Parry, although returning at a far slower pace, had beaten him to the meadow and the two officials were re-adjusting the stumps and bails on the empty wicket as the lad turned the corner towards the pavilion. He was more than a little annoyed at being first back, and hardly surprising either.

Young toddlers screamed with delight as dogs barked at tormenting adults, but the wicket was silent. Where on earth had his team-mates got to? He reduced his speed and shortened his pace, delighted not to let the side down through absenteeism. Then both sides appeared only a minute or so behind Julian, chuckling their way back from the boozer. They fell around like men returning to their coach on a factory beano, not legless but jovial nonetheless. Down the road they huddled and pushed like greyhounds at Walthamstow Stadium. They passed the stray Julian in mid-joke so he had to wait a while for their acknowledgement . . . .

'So this geezer, right, he goes into the dentist's shop, right, and this toothpicker says to him we don't do nothing on the National Health, right? Only private. So, he says you can have all your teeth out with a proper anaesthetic and there'll be no blood or nothing and that will cost you a hundred quid. Or you can have half your 'ampsteads done, a little bit of blood and that will cost fifty quid. Failing that, he says, we can knock the teeth out with a sledge 'ammer and there'll be blood pouring out the gums, and that'll cost a quid. So this geezer says I'll have the last one for a quid and can you book the wife in for eleven o'clock tomorrow morning?'

The Creek cricketers fell to the floor in raptures, but the Little Dow players merely smiled politely, having missed much of the point because of translation difficulties. The East Enders hugged their guts as though appendicitis had attacked them. Then they noticed the presence of their opening bowler. Julian smiled at their belated welcome. He hadn't bowled particularly well by his standards, but had scored rather well since lunch had been called. His jealous team-mates knew it too as they read through his wry grin of satisfaction.

'You jammy bastard!' snarled one.

'How was it then?' asked Winston, who thought he should know these things as he was the skipper. 'Was it that horse and cart on the boundary with the yellow jumper on?' he asked.

'I can't remember,' replied Julian sarcastically, 'she

didn't have a stitch on last time I saw her.' Julian chuckled mildly as he looked at the envious faces of his frustrated pals.

Aubrey Padgett, groundsman, scorer and pavilion painter, used a light roller on the wicket. Nearly a dozen times he followed his own tracks as he smoothed down the bumpy particles which the spikes of the cricket boots had lifted from the wicket. He was very hot . . . he removed his trusty sweater to reveal a traditional collarless shirt, which disguised an extravagant tattoo declaring how much Aubrey loved Joan. Who would have thought such a frail, pathetic man could risk such abuse of his frame to commemorate a woman whom he hadn't seen for over twenty-five years? But there it was for all to see, plain as a pikestaff — 'I Love Joan' — from elbow down to wrist encased in the wings of a Wedgwood-blue vulture or eagle. The spectators chose not to comment as he pushed and pulled the old horse roller to and fro, from pavilion end to oak-tree end and back again. His tattoo hinted at a murky past to inquisitive members of the village fraternity but nobody really cared.

He rested the heavy rusting beast against the left-hand, peeling wall of the changing rooms, well aware the weather boarding face-on would have creaked and groaned under the immense weight. Then he returned to the square, armed with a galvanised bucket from which the handle had mysteriously strayed, filled to the brim with whitewash that was in truth hardly white. The bucket had housed much dirt through the spring and the white paint had tinted to a 'lively beige'. It resembled a mammoth cauldron of cream of mushroom soup. In his other hand Aubrey held a balding plasterer's brush and a metal strip stencil for his straight edge.

The attraction of the working man was as curious as ever as the observing spectators munched, boozed and basked their way towards the afternoon session, studying the energetic routine of the groundsman. It was hardly the warmest day of the year, and even the bravest player still sported a short-sleeved sweater, but the whitewash dried instantly in the afternoon breeze and Aubrey dripped like a sponge lifted from a bathtub. However, the crease looked immaculate.

The polite on-lookers applauded the drenched chap all the way back to the pavilion where he automatically demolished a large dosage of orange squash without it touching either side of his mouth. Aubrey, poor Aubrey, suddenly felt wretched. It was, after all, the player's drink for the afternoon session. What if Peter Jackson found out? What on earth would he say? Perhaps Aubrey would be relieved of his duties? Nevertheless the frightened man would run the gauntlet, because his throat had felt like the bottom of a budgie's cage. He pulled himself together and went outside to rearrange the tin numbers that lay scattered around like cards in a snap session. He opened the scorebook at the relevant page, patted his rib-cage for a fountain pen and took up his rightful position adjacent to the pavilion steps.

Slogger Stevenson and Eddie Peters practised their batting strokes beside him bored with standing for hours in the outfield with not so much as a sniff of a catch. Winston tossed them a few tame off-break teasers while Monty, pads and all, sent down a few spin balls of astonishing accuracy. Slogger Stevenson looked keen to live up to his name, scattering humans and animals alike around the boundary ropes. Stevenson, being a foundry worker at Ford's Dagenham plant, was a mighty strong man, more than capable of knocking a few sixes, even tens or twelves had such shots existed. He flayed the ball around with much ease but little style. His strokeplay was about as subtle as a road accident but he could hit a few runs when he felt like it. He was usually stumped or caught on the ropes, occasionally trapped leg before, but nobody could recall his ever being bowled out. For the moment, though, he had to make do with returning to the outfield. The Little Dow batsmen were padded up and ready to return to the middle.

'Come on, lads, game on, best of order,' yelled Winston to his bat-happy clan. 'We're still fielding, don't forget. Get them plates of meat moving and get out there. I want to be batting in an hour. Come on, lads,' he chanted with clapping hands.

Peter Jackson completed his pep talk to his undefeated batsmen, Geoffrey Baird and Philip Trevelyan, and strolled across to remind himself of the exact situation. Aubrey Padgett leaned over, allowing the captain he worshipped to study the immaculate scribing.

Baker J.	*ct Donald*	*b Jannik*	*16*
Baker B.		*b Waites R.*	*1*
Baird	*not out*		*51*
Jackson	*ct Pinder*	*b Waites W.*	*7*
Copeland	*ct Holt*	*b Waites R.*	*2*
Trevelyan	*not out*		*2*
extras			*6*
TOTAL			*85 for 4 wickets*

Jackson gave a contented nod of thanks to Padgett for letting him glimpse his work of art. He turned around to see the back of Geoffrey Baird (something he had wanted to see for years) who was setting off for the crease. Then he strolled behind the pavilion in search of a relief location. There, he cleared his system of the few pints of best bitter he had absorbed during conversation at the Plough. He tramped into the undergrowth where a giant blackberry bush, wild but yielding, concealed him from the allotment tenders.

Mrs Robbins had decided to make tea for the batting side as well as the vicar, who had called in to give the game his blessing. She wandered round to the back of the pavilion in search of a suitable place to empty the spent tea leaves from the massive alloy pot. Her eyes met Jackson's and she dropped the teapot.

'Mr Jackson, I don't think I've seen the likes before in my whole life,' she chuckled.

'Oh, how nice of you to say so,' replied the flattered solicitor.

'Well I never,' she mused.

'Two lumps,' he whispered with a sheepish grin, removing the offending member from sight, and raising his zip to a level of respectability. Then he strolled around to the front yelling good luck gestures to the departing Trevelyan.

'Keep the bat straight and the score moving along. Right-o?'

Mrs Robbins returned to the tea room within the pavilion grasping the empty but newly dented teapot. She had turned a whiter shade of pale.

'My dear, what in heaven's name has happened? You look like you've just seen a ghost,' said her neighbour.

'Well, it wasn't exactly a ghost, Alice . . . let's just say that in a rather strange sort of a way my younger days flashed before me.'

'Go on,' retorted the cheeky Alice.

The fielding side had taken up the positions they had reluctantly vacated for the public house, and applauded in the two batsmen, keen to wipe out Baird before he did much more damage. Half a century was humiliating. It was no fun any longer. A matter of principle. Winston closed in his field a little, ten men eager to capture the sacred scalp of the in-form batsman and the solitary Julian Jannik, far too knackered to remember which of the two batsmen *was* Geoffrey Baird. Waites tossed the ball to Julian, who was less enthusiastic than usual, but having felt the ball in his grasp his eagerness returned and he prepared himself for the first delivery. He rubbed the ball furiously as Baird studied the outfield. Julian had a quick glance around too, but to no avail, she must have still been sound asleep. Parry Taylor dropped his arm as Baird crouched, tapping the crease eagerly.

'Play,' called Parry.

Montgomery Holt crouched and the remainder of the fielders followed suit. Some had drunk maybe half a gallon too much but good old Julian hadn't touched a drop. He ran in and the afternoon session was under way.

'Well, what can I say, when Mrs Robbins appeared behind that pavilion. You could have knocked me down with a feather. It was embarrassing for both of us. I mean to say, that old woman had known me since I went to primary school. For her to witness such a thing was, as I say, embarrassing. The other problem was that I was so surprised when she appeared, I lost my direction and jolly well flooded the front of my flannels. Red dye is quite acceptable on cricket flannels, but I'm not sure about anything else.

Geoffrey had batted well before lunch and I felt we needed a good knock from him to secure a decent score. I strolled by the scoreboard, passing an open window of the pavilion. Mrs Robbins was washing cups, peering through the hole in the weather boarding.

"Oh, Mrs Robbins, are you all right now?" I asked her.

"Yes I'm fine, Mr Jackson, if a little surprised."

"Surprised?" I asked her, "Surely you couldn't have been that taken back. I mean to say, Mrs Robbins, you must have seen it all before?"

"No, I'm afraid I haven't . . . not all of it . . . and I'm surprised because I pick those blackberries every year to make jam for the church fête, and you've made me wonder how many other kind folk have, well, tampered with them."

Mrs Robbins flushed prettily and went about her duties in the pavilion, where she had cakes, cups and sandwiches to prepare.

I puffed at my old pipe and sat on the boundary hoping to see some good action. Julian had looked good during the morning session. I hoped that he would eventually cock something up — not knowing at the time he already had.'

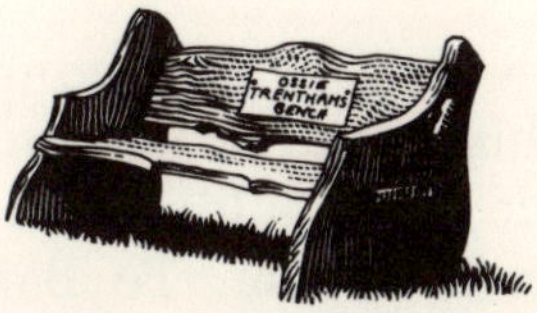

— THREE —

The Afternoon Session

Geoffrey Baird never went to Wednesday evening nets, only ever lifting his bat to score runs. Net practice was riddled with people who couldn't bowl, flinging deliveries to people who couldn't bat. To Baird it was a totally worthless exercise, a complete waste of a spring or summer evening.

Julian Jannik's curved run was almost complete, his heart and legs pounding in unison with the soft patting of the bat by the eager Baird. Parry Taylor stared at the bowler's crease as the combined volume of heavy breathing, boots on grass and ruffling shirt and flannels passed by his left ear. A fair run-up, the official adjudged, so he raised his head to watch the delivery. The first ball of the afternoon session passed as harmlessly as a cloud overhead. Winston had forecast that Julian would dish out a lot of trouble, and the weather man on the previous evening's news had forecast rain. Both had been inaccurate. A hat-trick of tame deliveries passed through to Monty, as extrovert as ever behind the wicket. Peter Jackson hoped his batsman was only getting his eye in —

to leave three consecutive deliveries well alone in a one-day match was tactically dubious. Julian looked tight on line and length, and his good bowling encouraged conscientious fielding from his team-mates. Baird had to open up sooner or later and they were in wait.

Superlatives were hardly necessary when describing Mr Baird. He looked as bland as his occupation, as characterless as his four-bedroomed bungalow beyond the oak trees. But cricket has never been a game of the untutored, as John Arlott once said, and public school had made a pretty fine cricketer out of a foolish man.

The sun burst through at twenty-five minutes to three. Baird immediately produced his cap from the back pocket of his flannels, a cap which resembled a cornish pasty by the way it had been folded. He lifted his bat as Julian leapt into the air before hurtling the ball at him. Baird instinctively stepped forward a solitary pace and as the ball scorched off the cropped strip he raised his head and cracked the ball with all his might. Belatedly he knelt on his front pad to add panache to the stroke. He turned his head expecting to see a blur in the distance, only to see the shot trickle to the right of mid-off for a single.

'Come on, run then,' shrieked Trevelyan.

'Just the one then,' commanded the disappointed Baird.

The crowd applauded the first run of the session, Julian removed some sort of lump from the spikes of his boot and Monty took the return to the stumps cleanly. Aubrey Padgett wriggled in his chair, making himself comfortable for the job in hand. Baird pulled his cap down despite having run into the shadows cast by the giant elms at right-angles to Lord Smythe's wall. It was the thing to do so he did it. Slogger Stevenson belched rudely as Trevelyan took middle and leg. Two balls remained of the over, then one and then . . . .

'Over,' called Parry Taylor, juggling with his temporarily redundant stones. 'Well bowled,' he whispered to Julian.

'Cheers, my son,' replied the cheeky Cockney to the

man old enough to be his grandfather. There was no animosity though, not between two men who loved the game so much. Parry recalled great moments in the game, moments of bygone days when Julian was merely knee-high to a grasshopper. That final triumphant test at the Oval in August 1963; the thrill of excitement when the capacity crowd surged forward in the final minutes to mob the outstanding Frank Worrell and his West Indian side — scenes forever committed to a golden page in the annals of the game. And the following year when Fiery Fred achieved those almost impossible bowling figures. (Sadly, Julian couldn't think back that far, because his brain was clogged up with his recent session of sexual delight.) Thirty years earlier Parry Taylor had played long stop at his local recreation ground, throwing a coat over the faster balls to save four byes. He limped off to square leg and Julian swaggered off to the mid-wicket boundary, his eyes scanning the crowd for his new heart-throb.

Lily Grace stomped authoritatively to her rightful position, the vast expanse of floral dress protruding beneath her white coat of officialdom. Winston and Rudi chatted for a moment as their paths crossed, Winston rubbing the ball furiously on his thigh before tossing it to his brother. Rudi fancied his chances more coming down the slight slope from the pavilion end.

Reginald Smythe had dined at the manor in the accustomed manner on fresh orange juice and strawberries. He loved attempting to play cricket for it enabled him to mix with his fellow villagers. Owning the meadow he allowed himself the odd luxury such as returning a few moments late from the luncheon period, or fielding in the sacred slips. He always bowled the last over of the innings too, had done for twelve years, and had never taken a single wicket. His tardiness was scarcely crucial, everyone knew Creek wouldn't declare under a hundred runs. Lord Smythe donated the village knockout cup, a popular event around the county, and this excused his very bad batting.

Surprisingly Lady Smythe had accompanied her husband back to the meadow. She relaxed on a sun bed, her superfluous sun-glasses perched on the top of her head, St Tropez style. Smutsy chose not to watch the tense proceedings out in the middle; there was little point considering he knew few of the rules. He preferred to scan the columns of 'Hunting and Fishing' in search of a new toy and sat in his Range Rover with the windscreen shielding him from the nippy afternoon breeze. The sun tried hard to appear for a few overs but Reginald Smythe did not notice. Crowd and players alike admired the custom-built convertible wagon, as impressive as a processional coach carrying Royalty. He had learned to ignore the admiring glances. He tried hard to be one of the lads, though preferred not to change in the filthy pavilion, nor to nibble those wretched pilchard things at the tea interval. Well, there were far more satisfying alternatives back at the manor. He carried his own bat and a personal highest knock of 7 not out. A vehement admirer of Cowdrey and all the man stood for, Lord Smythe had personally dropped a line to the cricketer to express his personal remorse at the then forty-two year old's decision to rejoin the ranks of Test cricket in Australia. Jeff Thomson, master surfer and part-time cricketer, had completely shattered the Cinderella return, causing the great legend to lay itself to rest for a second time. Cowdrey was disappointed with that tour and Lord Smutsy was devastated, yet he still imagined himself as his Kentish hero when he took up his position at second slip. It was a generous gesture to him, for he chose never to practise his catching with the rest of the side before play commenced. It seemed a pointless practice to him, and his only attempt had resulted in stinging hands.

Rudi Waites stormed in with a yard extra pace to resume his fierce attack on Geoffrey Baird. The first ball shot well wide and Lily signalled so, showing her suspender straps in the process.

'Gorblimey, look at that,' said Eddie to Slogger.

'I thought you were into that sort of thing,' chuckled his chum.

'You're joking. Them sort of suspenders could hold up the bleedin' Severn Bridge.'

The two laughed before returning to their original placements on the boundary. Rudi cursed his pathetic delivery, while Baird tapped his box to ensure that all was in good working order.

Geoffrey Baird homed in on the next delivery through his tinted specs and stroked a fine four through the covers. Two spectators scattered as the leather missile sped towards them, and the rest applauded a brilliant shot.

'Stay there,' yelled Winston to Alfie Donald, who had kindly sprinted off to retrieve the ball from the overgrown community of fading daffodils and crocuses. Donald acknowledged the command and threw the ball with all his might back to the bowler. It bounced five times before being helped on its way by Stevie Whiteman.

Baird added a few more runs to his score before the over was complete. Rudi Waites was disgusted with his bowling and his team-mates were silent, aware of the problem Winston had, for if neither Julian nor Rudi could Creek would have great difficulty in bowling out such a proficient batsman.

Julian, tight as ever yet rarely penetrative, bowled another maiden and Trevelyan took a few more off Rudi, who took his sweater voluntarily from Lily Grace and sulked his way to mid-on.

Baker B.	*ct Donald*	*b Jannik*	*16*
Baker J.		*b Waites R.*	*1*
Baird	*not out*		*60*
Jackson	*ct Pinder*	*b Waites W.*	*7*
Copeland	*ct Holt*	*b Waites R.*	*2*
Trevelyan	*not out*		*9*
extras			*7*
TOTAL			*102 for 4 wickets*

The crowd roared their approval at the achievement of three figures. Smutsy looked up, a little interest brewing. The batsmen chatted lightly in the middle, leaning on their bats like twin Towers of Pisa, delighted at their progress. They watched the fielders take up fresh positions for the new over. Winston stood beside Parry Taylor and Julian Jannik, determined to sort out a sloppy field that was allowing too many runs to get through. Julian walked back to his run-up position while his captain completely rearranged the field.

Meanwhile, Molly glanced at the travel clock on her mother's bedside cabinet. She retrieved her knickers from the bottom of the bed and unravelled the material, trying desperately to remember how the bed had been made before the trespass. She opened the bedroom window, releasing the slight giveaway smell of physical combat, and heard the distant applause for the hundred up. Her hair and clothes were all over the place but she brought both into ship-shape order, deliriously happy with her lunch interval. Like many people, she had never before believed in love at first sight, but having now made love at first sight, she now believed in it.

Julian Jannik was silent, waiting patiently as Winston moved his men like chess-pieces across the green board. Monty moved two feet closer to the stumps, a brave gesture as Julian had not the slightest intention of easing his pace. Winston himself would guard the wide area between keeper and second slip, and Rudi and Stevie Whiteman were at thirdish slip and gully respectively. Vince Clayton dropped back from a silly-point position to the covers on the off side, Winston hoping that his Viv Richards style of fielding would save a few crafty singles which the two batsmen had been chancing. Pumps Parker patrolled the ropes at long-off in front of the pavilion steps while Julian himself would run down to a silly mid-off area once he had bowled. Alfie Donald took charge of the remainder of the boundary on the off side, positioning himself somewhere between deep extra cover and the mid-wicket boundary. This left a gap between Stevie Whiteman and Clayton but provided Julian bowled a straight ball, it would need a damn good square-cut to get the ball away down in that region.

The on side offered only a token field, with Screwball Pinder resuming at mid-on and Slogger Stevenson and Eddie Peters deeper out, so any delivery on the leg side would be pulverised. That was the risk Winston had to take, what with the score creeping up each consecutive over.

Baird and Trevelyan had decided to go for it; with so many batsmen to follow it was worth taking a chance or two.

Julian had undoubtedly lost a little edge as he ran in and bowled to Trevelyan, a snick between the two slips, a gasp from the crowd and the ball was on its way to the outfield.

'Come on,' demanded Baird to the batsman who hadn't seen where his stroke had sent the ball.

'How many?' asked the grateful Trevelyan.

'Two if you like.'

'Unlucky, Julian,' called Winston as Rudi gave chase, avoiding the dog shit in slalom fashion.

'Sod it!' exclaimed the disconsolate Julian.

'I beg your pardon, young man?' exclaimed Lily.

'I said sod, sod it, SOD IT!' replied the bowler as Rudi flung the ball accurately into the waiting gloves of Monty, a fine throw that brought a ripple from those spectators who enjoyed the finer points of the game.

'Well I never did,' complained Lily Grace, who was disgusted by the crude comments that littered the field. She was a firm and proper woman in an age of progressive barbarism. She had always felt there was ample opening for guardians of public behaviour, and never more needed than is this particular game.

'Come on, lads, on the old buttons and bows now,' demanded Winston. Trevelyan played a few safety strokes to regain his composure until, on the last ball of the over, the blood rushed to his head and he skied an immense shot to the mid-wicket boundary. Alfie Donald ran round about twenty yards before taking a beautiful catch on the drop. The Creek side danced and dangled in mid-air like crazed Tavern boozers and then raced to congratulate Donald's second catch of the innings. It was a good catch, no doubt about it, and he seemed to wallow complacently in the hugs of congratulations rather more than he ought.

Philip Trevelyan was out; Jannik had wanted to see the back of Baird (as indeed did most of the villagers) but Trevelyan would do for a start. The unfortunate batsman had looked set for a good knock; his ability was unquestionable, his application questionable, his pedigree unquestionable and his previous scores questionable. His father, too, had played for Little Dow before he was cut down before his prime at the tender age of forty-four. The Trevelyans were cricket-mad and thus derived much pleasure from finding a suitable epitaph for Trevelyan senior:

Here lies young Harry
Who was never that strong.
Although a good long stop
He didn't stop long.

Philip Trevelyan pretended his father watched whenever he was at the crease, and as he left the field he raised his head to the heavens to apologise for such an artistically-minus knock. The polite on-lookers once more clapped in the defeated striker but there was no raise of a bat or tip of a cap. Tom Tarry crossed Trevelyan about twenty feet from the boundary.

'Good luck to you, young lad.'

'Thanks Mr Trevelyan, is it turning out there?'

'No, but the wicket-keeper's been eating garlic. Most off-putting. Mind how you go now, keep the bat straight.'

'Will do.'

'Good knock, Philip,' cried a villager.

'Here, here,' seconded another.

'I was more than sorry to see Philip Trevelyan dismissed so early on, as he was a kind man who lived for his village cricket. His personal best for us was 103 against Trent Copham the season before I was nominated captain, but it had been an indifferent season for the mild-mannered chap.

I was interested to see how young Tom Tarry would cope with such fierce bowling. Julian what's-his-name had the bit between his teeth and it was obvious the next ball would be a corker if not a yorker. I noticed Baird signalling for a glass of water, but I, along with the rest of the gathering, chose to ignore the arrogant fellow. I fancied pointing Percy at the porcelain but had no idea where Mrs Robbins was, and twice in one day would have been quite unforgivable. Besides, I had to see how Tom Tarry would fare against Julian.'

The engrossed throng sportingly clapped Julian's wicket. Trevelyan walked across, one pad dismantled, the other still attached to his leg, to check on his score. Aubrey Padgett turned the book around to show the victim his final tally.

Baker B.	*ct Donald*	*b Jannik*	*16*
Baker J.		*b Waites R.*	*1*
Baird	*not out*		*60*
Jackson	*ct Pinder*	*b Waites W.*	*7*
Copeland	*ct Holt*	*b Waites R.*	*2*
Trevelyan	*ct Donald*	*b Jannik*	*12*
Tarry	*not out*		*0*
extras			*8*
TOTAL			*106 for 5 wickets*

Rudi Waites clenched the ball with a finger each side of the seam in traditional style, his thumbnail rubbing across the same. He turned to face Baird. Parry Taylor dropped his arm . . . game on . . . best of order, and Rudi jogged in at a slow to medium pace. The ball never turned and its extra length enabled the old campaigner to meet it on the half volley, sending it screaming to the off-side boundary for four superbly executed runs. Rudi applauded the shot.

'Give me another ball like that, old son, and you'll be clapping another boundary,' remarked the supercilious Baird.

'What did you say, man?' enquired the disbelieving Londoner.

'I can wallop them all round the meadow. Do you have any more?'

'Get stuffed!' suggested Rudi and measured a few extra paces on to the tail-end of his run.

The unflappable Baird prodded at the popping crease, unaware of the daggers that were flying at him from all quarters. Rudi sprinted in, the whites of his eyes glaring, and the ball left his hand as if propelled by a nuclear catapult. It was a short ball and reared up viciously. Baird leapt backwards, trying to play the ball down, but the ball shot sixty degrees or so into the air. It was snapped up by Winston Waites somewhere between first and second slip and the damaging demon Baird was on his way back to the pavilion. The brothers had drawn blood, and at that moment Rudi wished it had not been only of the metaphorical variety.

'Good ball, my friend,' commented Baird a little too deliberately as he passed the bowler.

'Bollocks!' replied the ecstatic Rudi Waites.

The players crowded around him and slapped his back gleefully. The danger man had gone and both sides were delighted. It had been a costly ploy to trap the number three, but he was well and truly returning to the pavilion. The spectators stood as he left the field, his pads chaffing together, bat tucked under his arm like an air marshall with his baton. Aubrey Padgett filled in the necessary details by Baird's name as the sporting victim threw his bat against the pavilion wall. A photograph of the 1957 unbeaten village side fell to the floor, shattering the musty glass into hundreds of pieces. He slammed his pads on top of the cricket bag and his gloves went more or less the same way. Damn good sport Baird.

> 'It is true that the game of cricket is loaded with drama and breathtaking incident, embellished by those classic moments when the all-time greats achieved peerless records; for instance when Botham hit out at the Australian attack like a crazed baseball player; or when Jim Laker took more wickets in one match than was ever thought sensible. But great moments of a game are often personal to the spectator, small and intimate, rather than flamboyant and headlined. It was nice to see that pompous Geoffrey quashed by a superb delivery, it was entertaining to see him caught, but I would have preferred to have seen him stay out there a little longer. Talk about sitting on the fence.'

The onus was on in-coming batsman Trevor White. He and the apprentice Tom Tarry were hardly forces to be reckoned with. Jackson looked quite distressed once he had rid his face of the grin that had appeared at the dismissal of Geoffrey Baird.

Trevor fended a few useful deliveries to see himself and his partner safely through to the end of the over. Fielders and spectators clapped, even cheered, Rudi Waites for a splendid touch of bowling. Trevor and Tarry met in the middle for the customary pow-wow.

'What do you reckon?' asked Trevor.

'About what?' young Tarry replied.

Trevor shrugged. 'Don't know really. Reckon the ball's turning?'

'Probably, but I haven't faced a delivery yet.'

'Do you reckon you can hold out?' asked the concerned Trevor.

'Probably . . . for two or three balls,' replied the nervously humorous Tarry to his elder.

Things didn't look too promising for Little Dow.

'What guard would you like, young man?' enquired Lily Grace maternally.

'Middle and leg, please,' he requested.

Tom Tarry edged his bat backwards and forwards waiting to be told that it was in the right position. He was terrified — even taking guard was a great strain, what with his bat quivering like a jelly.

'That is middle and leg, young man,' Lily assured him.

'Thank you very much.'

Lily was quite delighted, never having been thanked for giving guard before. Tarry tapped at the popping crease, not bothering to glance around at the field. If he hit the ball he would blooming well run.

Julian Jannik pushed his wide shoulders forward and sprinted towards the crease. Tarry's knees shook behind the pads, and his eyes squinted in premature fear of focusing on the approaching guided missile. Julian shot into the air and his arm spun like a windmill in a hurricane. Tarry bravely stepped forward as the ball came his way, played across the line and felt a dreadful thud on his front pad.

'Owzat!' screamed Julian in good humour, knowing full well the young lad was far too far forward to be dismissed. Monty went up with him for the crack, but nobody else seemed particularly bothered.

'Yes, that's out,' confirmed Lily Grace.

'What for?' exclaimed the bemused Tarry.

'For the whole afternoon,' snapped the umpress.

'You have to be ruddy joking. That was never out in a month of Sundays,' said Trevor White.

Julian Jannik looked in disbelief first at the umpire and then at Tarry's front leg and then back at the umpire. The young batsman was absolutely devastated. Lily raised her finger and that was that.

'That was never out, man,' Julian told her.

'Then you shouldn't have appealed. I'm giving you the

benefit of the doubt. Truly it was close but I'll give you the decision,' the unconcerned Lily explained.

'Here, Julian, watch it my son, she probably wants you to give her one,' yelled Screwball Pinder from mid-on.

'Enough, thank you,' demanded Lily.

So the dejected Tom Tarry was out first ball. He walked from the strip slowly with a glare that hushed the whole meadow. Parry Taylor coughed at square leg, praying he wasn't to be consulted over the decision. Lily had blundered, no doubt about that, but it was such a shame it had to be the young lad playing in his first senior fixture.

Peter Jackson walked to meet poor Tom as he returned to the pavilion. He saw the tears welling in the boy's eyes, and put his arm around the slender frame. The crowd applauded the young lad harder than they had Geoffrey Baird. Lily checked her number of stones and tried hard to whistle, though not a solitary note had passed between her rounded and scarlet lips for over a quarter of a century. She glanced up at the looming clouds overhead, preferring to ignore the giggling fielders.

It had been a dreadfully hard decision to give Julian Jannik his third wicket of the day, but he wasn't that sure that he wanted it. Rudi and Winston were fine sportsmen, although a little immature at times admittedly, and they together with the successful bowler spoke sternly at the crease as Tarry walked off heartbroken, propped up by his captain. The boy's bat was slung superfluously under his arm as he nibbled at the tips of his batting gloves. The crowd's applause was little consolation.

'Did you see that, Mr Jackson?' he asked.

'Certainly did, Tom old boy.'

'If that was out then I'm richer than Lord Smythe,' the boy gurgled in saddened tones. 'My front leg was well forward, and that old bag couldn't possibly have known if the ball was about to turn. It's disgusting, if you ask me, makes you want to either give the game up or go and smack her round the head with a cricket bat.'

'I'm afraid, Tom old boy, the umpire's decision is always final and so long as it is a game of gentlemen, then you must abide by each decision and accept even the wayward ones with dignity. Smacking an umpire round the head is hardly advisable, especially in this case . . . that bat you were using cost the club over forty quid . . . hardly want that to go the way of the west, do we now?'

The boy smiled at the remark and raised his head for the first time since the official finger had been raised. Peter Jackson took his arm away from the boy's shoulder, leaving the young lad to walk staunchly back to the pavilion.

'Take those pads off, lad, and go and ask Mrs Robbins for a nice cup of tea, and then get yourself some bowling practice. After all, that's what you are in the side for, isn't it? Not your batting.'

'Bloody good job too,' agreed the youngster. 'Got a ciggy, Mr Jackson?'

'Only smoke a pipe, old man, sorry.'

'Never mind, didn't really want one anyway.'

Peter Jackson pondered on more important things as Nicholas O'Connor strolled out to the wicket, being met halfway by an anxious Trevor White.

'Any news from the skipper about a declaration or anything?' asked Trevor ambitiously.

'Not enough runs for that, Trev. Keep a straight bat and run on what we can. We'll be all right so long as we keep our heads.'

Molly walked sprightly from her parent's gingerbread cottage, wearing less underclothing than she had worn in the morning but more than she had at lunchtime.

It was getting a little chillier. There was a bit of a 'George Raft' as the Creek lads put it, and as Molly turned off the main road down the towpath towards the meadow her nipples shot up like hot toast. However, nobody was around to notice, at least not until she reached the bend of the river where anglers lay in wait of something or other. Molly had enjoyed making love with Julian, and Julian had too, so it was inevitable they would collide once more before eventide fell upon the village like a royal blue curtain. She chose to ignore the appreciative wolf whistles of the pot-bellied angling fraternity as she passed; dirty old men should have known better. She shuddered at the thought of those filthy fingers that filled the whistling mouths, the very same digits that had affixed worm or maggot to hook for the last six or seven hours. Molly remembered the corny gag about the two maggots making love in dead Ernest, chuckled to herself and turned away from the river towards the on-side mid-wicket boundary. The anglers turned back to the river in time to see floats reappearing without bait beneath and rod top still after a tell-tale quiver.

'Oh sod, missed it,' complained one.

'Nice tits eh?' said another, rebaiting with a fresh maggot.

'Don't interest me, old son,' retorted angler number one.

'Nor me,' said the other, followed by 'not bleeding much' under his breath.

Julian Jannik stood rubbing the ball at deepish mid-off, chatting blandly to the bland Pumps Parker. Molly sat herself down at the boundary ropes, surprising Julian as he turned to take up his running position upon the arrival of new batsman O'Connor.

'Hi,' called Julian softly. 'How you feeling?'

'Content,' she replied.

'Not too content I hope?' asked the rascal.

'OK then, not too content. How you doing?'

'Taken three wickets so far, darling. Well, two and a half really, the last guy was never out but the umpire gave it to me,' he admitted.

'Gave what to you?' asked Molly sarcastically.

'Never mind, never mind.'

Nicholas O'Connor took guard on his middle and leg stumps, but Molly was thinking more of middle and leg-over.

Two balls to come: Julian to O'Connor. Play.

The black athlete sprinted in on his curved run and sent such a stunning delivery through O'Connor's guard that the ball shot away for two leg-byes. O'Connor was delighted, unable to recall the last time he had called for two runs, leg-byes or not. Two more extras slipped themselves on to the grand total and then it was the final ball of the over. Winston didn't seem to care who would receive strike at the beginning of the next over, so he chose not to change his field. Julian to O'Connor, a crack of wood on leather and it was a well-taken single, wide of point. O'Connor was off the mark and Aubrey Padgett updated the details in the scorebook:

Baker B.	*ct Donald*	*b Jannik*	*16*
Baker J.		*b Waites R.*	*1*
Baird	*ct Waites W.*	*b Waites R.*	*64*
Jackson	*ct Pinder*	*b Waites W.*	*7*
Copeland	*ct Holt*	*b Waites R.*	*2*
Trevelyan	*ct Donald*	*b Jannik*	*12*
Tarry	*LBW*	*b Jannik*	*0*
White	*not out*		*0*
O'Connor	*not out*		*1*
extras			*10*
TOTAL			*113 for 7 wickets*

Julian strolled wearily back to the boundary and winked at Molly, Nicholas O'Connor screwed up his eyes and looked at the heavens, Trevor White practised a really dreadful shot by the side of Parry Taylor, and Vince Clayton picked his nose aggressively in the gully. A declaration was hardly in order with so few runs on the board, so it was time for young Winston to start putting pressure on his boss's side. Four slips, a leg slip, fine silly point and gully all gathered around O'Connor's bat.

Change of bowling, Alfie Donald, right arm over.

Donald took just three paces before reaching the crease and letting fly his unique style of delivery. It was neither fast, medium nor slow, but it *was* appallingly short. Had O'Connor not stepped forward the ball would have bounced twice before meeting a defensive stroke off the back leg. O'Connor, however, was in swashbuckling mood, even if his plan to score many runs was as unlikely as Graham Dilley's half-century at Headingley against the Aussies. The ball left his bat like grapeshot, flying through the air and bouncing only once before colliding with Lord Smythe's perimeter wall. Six runs. Parry Taylor's arms shot high in the air as O'Connor asked for confirmation of the first long-hop six of his lengthy career. The spectators roared their approval, and Aubrey Padgett came close to a hernia, his right hand scribbling nine to the dozen.

'Keep it tight, man,' demanded Winston.

'Sorry, Win,' whimpered the guilty bowler. 'Ball must have slipped, I reckon.'

'OK man, just keep it tight,' replied the concerned skipper.

In came Donald to O'Connor — one loosener was quite acceptable, even at the highest levels of the game, but never two. Donald strove for line and length. His right arm came down hard from above his head, giving the delivery so much momentum that he farted as he released the ball. O'Connor smacked the ball straight back at the bowler, and had Donald not turned to apologise to Parry Taylor he would have been able to boast a glorious caught and bowled. Instead, the ball screamed wide of Pumps Parker and disappeared in the long grass to the right of the pavilion for four more runs.

Ten runs off two balls and O'Connor in double figures; the game seemed to be undergoing an entirely different complexion. Donald was cheesed off but not to the extent of his captain, who had taken the gamble of bringing on a little spin and seemed to be losing. Half the excited spectators were on their feet praising the reluctant and unexpected hero. Jackson was delighted, and Donald and his side, who had previously sensed victory, were suddenly feeling apprehensive.

After only a few minutes at the crease, Nicholas O'Connor, a bowler who kept the ball as tidy as Mike Hendrick yet sadly who batted like Mike Hendrick also, was seeing the little red missile like a glorious football. He completely missed the third ball (a blessing for the windscreen of Lord Smythe's Range Rover) but the fourth he steered for two runs beyond the reach of the grasping Rudi. Winston gave chase and returned the ball wildly to Monty. The ball ricocheted off the keeper's gloves and spun away for a single overthrow. Another run to the jubilant O'Connor whose cluster of runs suddenly became a career best of 14 not out. Trevor got off the mark during the same over and O'Connor took another welcome run off a sloppy delivery.

It was all smiles when the two batsmen met between stumps at the end of the over. O'Connor had surpassed his career best, and Trevor White's single was his highest score for over a year. The spectators were told of these facts by an ecstatic Aubrey, and roared their approval.

Nicholas O'Connor to receive from the angered Julian Jannik, who was more than annoyed by Alfie Donald's six gifts to the opposition, and felt like making amends. O'Connor knew he had been lucky and knew he would be luckier still to be still out there, wicket intact, at the end of the next over.

Julian rubbed the ball curiously as he walked back to his own personal starting grid. Molly, misconstruing the movement, gaped with glee, but the bowler was too concerned with what was happening on the field to notice the wide eyes of admiration. A few shuffles and Julian was treading his well-trodden path once more, spikes churning out the outfield like stepping-stone foundations. He meant business and Nicholas knew it but stood firm at the other end. The attacker grunted loudly as he released another deadly ball and before O'Connor knew what was happening, the ball shot off a thin edge and rolled quickly away from the slip fielders. Two runs and O'Connor had had a reprieve.

Trevor took guard, looked around the field then lost his middle stump to a ball that beat him for line and speed. The thankful fielders leapt up in unison and the poor chap was on his way back to the pavilion, head bowed in disgrace. But it was a good ball, worthy of a good victim.

He dejectedly ambled towards the dressing-room, staring at the closely cropped outfield. He had analysed his dismissal for twenty or thirty yards but the reason for it was obvious to him; he simply wasn't bloody good enough. He didn't mind too much, because he was a good bowler and fancied himself to make amends when he got back out there. All the same, he went through the vanquished batsman's ritual of perplexity and regret with its trademark of a drooping head. He raised his eyebrows to acknowledge the clapping and noticed the two or three parasols that swayed the muddled breezes of June. Elderly couples in bowling-green sun-hats and fashionable wire-framed spectacles perched beneath the coloured canvas mushrooms astride wicker hampers, giving the general impression of the seafront at Eastbourne on a cold September evening.

A lowly starling scampered beyond the ropes in pursuit of an abandoned crisp packet. Such tiny legs carrying such a feathered girth. It scurried by like a portly Lord's Taverner, attracted by the cheese and onion fragrance.

One batsman awaited White's pads, another rescued his own personal bat, as Trevor removed his box. He conned a cigarette from Baker B., checked the progress on the tin numbers and settled to reflect on what wasn't nor was ever likely to be.

Lord Smythe hadn't batted for three matches, declarations having saved him the embarrassment. He never took guard, because he wasn't that certain of the purpose.

The field drew closer to the batsman, who despite his inability to play, looked rather splendid with the best padding and willow that money could buy. Smutsy's pads glistened in the grey afternoon; he wore thigh pads on both legs, something never seen on any other ground on that or any other day, and his portly belly also needed a pad, to be honest. His schoolboy cap perched ungainly on the top of his large head, his whiskers, falling from either side looking like a shortened hairy chinstrap. Lord Smythe looked fearfully on as Julian sprinted towards him like a crazed cannibal from the colonies. He raised his arm just as the bowler approached the mark, the umpire's arm shot up like a car park barrier and all was halted. Smythe waved for a young lad to be seated, the crowd looked about themselves in complete bewilderment and thirty seconds later, the runaway train hurtled from the outfield once more.

The ball skidded off the cropped grass and rose high towards the waiting recipient. His Lordship swung wildly at the ball but connected, much to the surprise of everybody.

'Run,' shrieked O'Connor.

'I beg your pardon?'

'Run, sir, you hit the ball.'

'Did I really?' asked the surprised tail-ender. 'Very well then, let's take one.'

'Two if you wish,' suggested O'Connor.

'I wish,' replied Smutsy, and had it not been for a disastrous misfield by the predictable Eddie Peters, a run-out would have been certain. Two runs to the meadow-owner who had loped with all the delicacy of a hippo on drugs. Smythe was delighted, his team-mates incredulous.

'For fuck's sake, Eddie, what are you doing, man?' asked the disconsolate bowler.

'Sorry, Julian, it hit a bump. Honest,' came the pathetic reply.

By the end of the over, Julian Jannik was despondent

and exhausted. It had been a long day both in the field and between the sheets and quite frankly he didn't fancy the Little Dow innings lasting much longer. His special tobacco was back in his kit-bag and he felt awful.

Lord Smythe always had a nose as red as a new ball, the trademark of an ardent sipper of malt whisky. He now had forehead and cheeks to match, two runs being too great an exertion for such an overweight frame. He huffed and puffed and looked more than a little disgruntled when he realised that the field was changing around to bowl at him once more.

'For God's sake, not again. I wish I hadn't bothered to run now.'

It had all been the fault of a leg-bye on the last ball of the over called by Nicholas O'Connor, and as the two unlikely batsmen met for an inquest Smythe looked concerned.

'Do I get that extra run?' asked Smythe.

'No, sir, that's a leg-bye,' replied O'Connor.

'Then I should be most grateful if you could leave the calling to me in future, young man. Understand?'

'Yes sir, of course, sir,' answered the man who knew which side his bread was buttered.

As it transpired the few sharp words were hypothetical for Rudi Waites, back after Alfie Donald's solitary six-ball disaster, dislodged the off stump with a tempting full toss that passed Smythe's defences with ease.

'I think his lordship is not in,' murmured O'Connor to himself.

Lord Smythe received tumultuous applause for his brace of runs. The villagers felt the aristocrat might spread more butter that way.

'Damn, just getting the old eye in there,' moaned Lord Smythe as he threw his bat down in disgust. 'Wicket looks good and true out there, Jackson. Thought I'd give it a crack. Right thing to do, eh?'

'Oh, of course, Smutsy,' replied Jackson sycophantically.

Spectators joined in the praise. 'Good knock, sir,' said one.

'Nobody could have got that one away,' said another.

'You fat slob,' whispered Molly as she peered at the pathetic man who was too overweight to strip off his own pads.

Aubrey Padgett completed the scorebook particulars and rushed off towards the pavilion to help the man he idolised and feared.

'Can I help, sir?' asked the scorer, groundsman and village handyman.

'Good fellow. Get that right pad off will you, Padgett, I'll do the gloves.'

'Very good, sir.'

Peter Jackson walked across and studied the stranded official scorebook. With only Joe Robbins left, things weren't looking too good for the home side. Joe was a far better player than Lord Smythe but ten times worse than any other player in the side — or in any other side for that matter.

Baker B.	*ct Donald*	*b Jannik*	*16*
Baker J.		*b Waites R.*	*1*
Baird	*ct Waites W.*	*b Waites R.*	*64*
Jackson	*ct Pinder*	*b Waites W.*	*7*
Copeland	*ct Holt*	*b Waites R.*	*2*
Trevelyan	*ct Donald*	*b Jannik*	*12*
Tarry	*LBW*	*b Jannik*	*0*
White		*b Jannik*	*1*
O'Connor	*not out*		*16*
Smythe		*b Waites R.*	*2*
Robbins	*not out*		*0*
extras			*11*
TOTAL			*132 for 9 wickets*

'As captain of Little Dow I had two options, to declare and boast that Creek Cricket Club never bowled us out, despite their superiority, or to hope that Lady Luck chose to flirt with Nicholas O'Connor for a few more overs. The middle order batsmen, myself included, had experienced one hell of a bad day, and in all fairness to that miserable Baird, he had set us off on the right route with his fine knock of sixty-four, even if he had thrown his wicket away when looking good for a ton. Tom Tarry was more than a little unfortunate with that unusual leg-before decision, but on the whole the umpiring had been first class so I had no real cause to complain. Julian Jannik and Winston's brother Rudi had done all the damage with some fine pace bowling, their physical attributes suggesting that they were good batsmen too. Quite honestly, I thought it was a bit of a slaughter. Joe Robbins in his day was one of the best batsmen ever to grace the Little Dow side, but at sixty-six one could hardly expect too much from the man. Provided he returned unharmed I would be more than satisfied.'

Joe Robbins took guard with a purpose and flair that belied his many years. The truth of the matter was that although he hadn't knocked up for the best part of one and a half seasons, he had scored three centuries in his earlier days with the village side.

Mrs Robbins momentarily ceased tossing tea bags into the giant pot like lumps of bread to hungry ducks and watched intently as her husband squared up for the first delivery from Rudi Waites. He took an off-stump guard, due to a troublesome right eye, and stood well square to the bowler. Mrs Robbins held her worried head in her hands as the big, black athlete turned and raced in towards her poor Joe. It was a tame delivery — Rudi respected the age of the number eleven batsman — and Robbins cracked it through extra cover off the back foot for four runs. A remarkable bonus for the down-and-out batting side. The crowd cheered like football fans, but Joe barely blinked. Rudi was furious as he came in a second time. The close fielders crouched and the tornado whipped up off the grass off a short length. The ball was kept down admirably.

'Stay!' yelled Robbins to all the village and surrounding area as well as to O'Connor who had no intention of running anyway.

'Right,' he called politely.

Joe prodded a worm that had had the audacity to cross the wicket and ruin his ailing concentration. The worm departed with a headache, Rudi shook his head with a smattering of heartache and Julian patrolled on the boundary with more personal aches than anybody.

That over went down in history and is often recalled on winter nights around the open fireplace of the Plough Hotel. How Joe Robbins took sixteen runs off the last four balls to crucify the talented Rudi Waites for twenty off the over. Joe played the strokes of a man possessed. The extra challenge had rekindled the old fire, and for those few minutes he reminded everyone of the player he had once been. They say an old cricketer never leaves the crease — indeed there is an older one probably lying beneath it. At the end of the over Rudi, who had so casually insulted Geoffrey Baird, went across and shook hands with the man who had ruined his day's figures. Two fine men in a tight grasp, exemplifying a gentlemen's game.

The on-lookers applauded them both and the change-over between overs seemed to take an eternity, which probably explained the dismissal of Nicholas O'Connor. He snicked a fine edge to Monty off an excellent Jannik delivery and that was the end of the innings.

Nobody wanted to blame O'Connor, for all his concentration had filtered away with Joe's marvellous twenty runs. The old man was clapped and cheered off the pitch by every person (including Geoffrey Baird) and he was even asked to sign two autographs.

Little Dow had lain down the gauntlet to the Creek side.

And that was the end of the Little Dow innings, all out for 152. Suddenly there was a game on and well the Creek boys knew it as they strolled off to discuss batting tactics. Julian apologised to Molly, explaining the necessity for him to be around at such an important team talk. Molly understood. Molly would have understood even if he had clubbed her with a Stuart Surridge long-handle.

Joe Robbins lit the Dutch cigar Lord Smythe had presented him with while lesser mortals threw the ball here and there in anticipation of a difficult couple of hours in the outfield. Jackson sent field instructions through the giant leather-padded fingers beneath his wicket-keeping gloves.

THE FINAL STATISTICS OF THE LITTLE DOW INNINGS

LITTLE DOW

BAKER B.	CT DONALD	B JANNIK	16	
BAKER J.		B WAITES R.	1	
BAIRD G.	CT WAITES W.	B WAITES R.	64	
JACKSON P.	CT PINDER	B WAITES W.	7	
COPELAND J.	CT HOLT	B WAITES R.	2	
TREVELYAN P.	CT DONALD	B JANNIK	12	
TARRY T.	LBW	B JANNIK	0	
WHITE T.		B JANNIK	1	
O'CONNOR	CT HOLT	B JANNIK	16	
SMYTHE, LORD		B WAITES R.	2	
ROBBINS J.	NOT OUT		20	
EXTRAS			11	
TOTAL			152	ALL OUT

CREEK CRICKET CLUB BOWLING FIGURES AND FIELDING ACHIEVEMENTS, NOT INCLUDING THE DROPPED CATCHES BUT INCLUDING THE MOST UNFAIR LEG-BEFORE-WICKET DISMISSAL

JANNIK J.	20 OVERS	2 MAIDENS	38 RUNS	5 WICKETS
WAITES R.	14 OVERS	1 MAIDEN	43 RUNS	4 WICKETS
WAITES W.	7 OVERS	0 MAIDEN	44 RUNS	1 WICKET
DONALD A.	1 OVER	0 MAIDEN	16 RUNS	0 WICKET

CATCHES

HOLT M.	2
DONALD A.	2
WAITES W.	1
PINDER S.	1

Yes, that was the strange thing about Aubrey Padgett, how upon completion of an innings he carefully erased his beautiful pencil work and replaced it with the flow from an italic fountain pen. Everything was in capital letters too, as though some great goal had been reached. His personal comments in the official headlines were characteristic.

Slogger Stevenson and his opening partner Eddie Peters walked menacingly to the middle as Peter Jackson, well aware of the few runs he had to play with, continued to boss and bully his fielders into astute positions, with the exception of Lord Smythe who took bossing and bullying from nobody, particularly as it was his meadow. Smutsy took up his rightful place at second slip, his Range Rover parked slightly beyond the mid-wicket boundary for easy access and quick exit. He stood patiently saying absolutely nothing, envious of his captain's knowledge of fielding positions without reference to notes or rule book. The rotund man of wealth wore a dazzling cap of green and yellow, not unlike a tame canary perched on the apex of his skull, and his immense stomach was hidden by a vast expanse of sweater, piped in matching shades.

Peter Jackson, confirmed wicket-keeper, was slightly more modern with his royal blue cap pushed down to his eyebrows, though occasionally he wore one of those white floppy hats which tend to make even the elegant and handsome David Gower appear somewhat vacant in the covers. His wasn't quite as absurd as the Phil Edmonds brimless variety, but it was silly all the same.

Little Dow had Peter Jackson behind the stumps with his pal and failed batsman, Barnaby Baker, by his side at first slip — forever his right-hand man. First slip was a cherished position in the field of village cricket and one that not necessarily went to the most deserving. Baker B. had obviously secured the place during strategic discussions in the first-class carriage that hurtled daily to Marylebone Station. Lord Smythe was next to him, blocking the sun from the gully. At silly point Philip Trevelyan flexed his muscles in preparation of a little ducking and diving for snicks off the thin edge. Thus stood the close fielders; two good players amongst them, favoured seniors clustered around the bat. Slips were the ultimate promotion (a type of cricket directorship) and lowly office boys and farm workers patrolled the boundary. Newcomers waited down at deep square leg, nervously anticipating a blisteringly painful catch from a square slam.

Trevor White was to open the bowling, quickly in to front-line duty as his wife had been some two or three hours previous. At the other end (of the wicket, that is, not the accommodating Mrs White) would be the on-form Nicholas O'Connor, a fast to medium bowler of proven ability.

Slogger Stevenson took guard and stubbed his fag-end out on the sole of his cricket boot, nearly drawing blood from his index finger as it scraped on a spike. He edged his bat towards middle and leg until Lily Grace assured him the bat had reached its destination. He tapped at the crease, disturbing the fresh line of whitewash, to find an existing trough excavated by a previous batsman. Gently prodding the perimeter he thereby received the first delivery at more or less middle stump. Twenty yards from him, at the bowler's end, Eddie Peters stood exceptionally wide from the crease, trying hard to lose the gut-trembling feeling caused by the waft of Lily's lavender water and talc. She looked more and more curious as his position from her position became more distant by the second. He looked a little pale and wan.

'Are you feeling all right, young man?' she asked kindly.

'Yeah, I'm all right, darling, it's the old currant bun,' he assured her, pointing to a slight tinge of yellow that was breaking through the grey afternoon sky.

'Oh really?' replied the unconvinced Lily Grace, rattling the six stones in her coat pocket. She raised her arm as Slogger Stevenson observed the field placings carefully.

'Ere,' Eddie asked, 'are you any relation to W.G. Grace?'

Before she could answer, the placid Trevor White interrupted, 'Yes, she's his grandmother,' then wished he hadn't.

Things were just about ready. Creek Cricket Club members lined the boundary rope directly in front of the pavilion, and ripe banter filled the still air, yet deep down even the most casual commentator wished Slogger and Eddie the best of luck as they set off in search of 153 glorious runs. Despite his yellow corduroy cricket flannels, Stevenson certainly looked the part of an opening bat, his head turning through the best part of a hundred and eighty degrees as he checked the unstopped gaps in the outfield. He glanced at Lord Smutsy in the slips.

'Safe area there,' he thought to himself. 'Worth a few square cuts, I reckon, cause it don't really matter if I get a thin edge, do it? Just so long as the edge ain't too thin like.'

His soliloquy ended as Trevor returned to the beginning of his run-up after a dummy charge to check his footings. Slogger patted the crease with his bat while Trevor wiped the new ball down the front of his trousers, unaware that his wife was probably fondling a similar region of a different pair of trousers somewhere in the village. He rolled up his sleeves, a sleeveless sweater for the first ball, off for the second — a time-honoured bowler's ritual.

'Go on, my son!' yelled Pumps Parker. 'Keep the old Jiminy intact, Slogger.'

'Twenty off the first over please, chaps,' requested Vince Clayton sarcastically.

Lily Grace took a last look over the field, her arm lowered and Creek's innings was under way. The meadow fell silent but for a few stray geese overhead in search of a quiet stretch of Thames, and for the butterflies kicking at Trevor White's stomach with such strength that he thought they'd borrowed a pair of Doctor Martin's from the opposition. He shuffled half a dozen times, leaned forward grasping the ball with his left hand and ran, gathering momentum as he neared the stumps. His run was slightly curved, John Snow fashion, his strides were long, Ken Higgs fashion, and his pace quite respectable by village standards of the game. His front foot slammed down on the crease with the power of a schoolboy yobbo murdering an innocent daddy-long-legs, while his back foot dragged forward. He gasped for that extra ounce of stamina as he leapt into the air sideways-on to the batsman, then his arm came down over his head towards the grass below. The ball was released with a grunt and it rocketed towards Slogger, scorching a minute area of cropped greenery en route. The seam sunk into the wicket and the ball turned away from the waiting batsman. Lily Grace stretched out her arms like a glider, Slogger offered no stroke to the first delivery and Peter Jackson danced across to save Barnaby Baker from a painful experience at first slip. It was a wide.

'Unlucky, Trevor old boy,' comforted the wicket-keeper.

'Yes, good length, Trevor,' seconded Lord Smythe aimlessly.

'That was fast,' observed Barnaby Baker, failed batsman.

'Shit!' uttered the wayward human catapult. By his standards it was a pathetic delivery. He studied his footmarks carefully as he strode by the umpire. Lily shuffled a stone from one pocket to another, then back again, realising six balls still remained after the wide delivery. Creek were off the mark.

If Trevor White hadn't combed his hair so regularly he would have resembled Dennis Lillee of Australia, not physically but facially. His black moustache hid his upper lip and his longish hair followed him through the run up before coming to rest on his shirt collar at silly mid-off.

When the mood took him, Slogger Stevenson could certainly bat well, as those spectators who had watched him warming up by the side of the pavilion could verify. Admittedly, Winston was only tossing friendly lobs to his opener but they were met with such ferocity that the crowd refused to take their eyes off the batsman for fear of a stray missile knocking off an unattentive head like a coconut at a fair.

The nets were discreetly positioned in the top left-hand corner of the meadow, if looking from the pavilion steps, tucked away where Lord Smythe's vast redbrick wall met the military-style line of oaks and elms. Purposefully well out of harm's way to prevent a stray ball from plumetting into a single thatched roof beyond the field, it was fortunate that Slogger Stevenson and Eddie Peters were unaware of the reason for the nets' location; they loved to get into harm's way. It was a long trek from pavilion to nets. The Creek lads decided not to make the assault, particularly padded up — it was hardly worth the bother.

Trevor White made amends for his shameful first ball by completing a tidy maiden. Little Dow, players and spectators alike, clapped a well-disciplined over. Winston Waites wasn't so impressed.

'What's up with Slogger, Rudi?' the captain murmured to his brother.

'Nerves, I think, man, this game suddenly means an awful lot to him. He don't wanna do nothin' stupid. There's a bit of grey matter in the old Uncle Ned after all, eh?'

'Looks like it, man,' agreed Winston. ''Ere Rudi, what's the time?'

Rudi looked at the jewelled waterproof, shockproof, and everything-else-proof clock on his arm.

'It's just gone a quarter to three.'

'Cheers. D'you know I think we're in for a few drops of the old sausages,' commented Winston in the most obscure Cockney rhyming slang.

'Bet ya a macaroni it don't?' offered Rudi with equal obscurity.

'You're on,' said Winston in near-perfect English, the deal secured with a handshake.

The Little Dow side had changed around for the next over, the first by the new boy Tom Tarry, a most generous gesture by Peter Jackson.

Tarry had more than impressed his skipper in practice sessions, and the slightly-built lad in his gleaming new whites looked quite confident as he stood discussing a few finer adjustments of the field. Parry Taylor had limped in from the square-leg position and was juggling one stone with one hand, occasionally raising his head to watch the various fielders move position to the young lad's demands. Parry was impressed, but the onlooking villagers around the ropes, most of whom had never seen the youngster before, were not so easily convinced.

Tom's new pumps pinched at his big toe (Jackson had guessed his size inaccurately) but he simply shortened his run. For his age Tom Tarry turned a ball quite menacingly, and either way too, just like Max Walker did. Tom was slight and vastly undernourished, whereas Walker, the highly underrated first-change bowler during the seventies Ashes series was burly and mustachioed, and always looked more like a hod-carrier than an athlete. The only hod-carrying Tarry was capable of was for Lego.

It was a delicately executed six balls from the new boy and after a dozen deliveries neither batsman had troubled the scorer. Rich applause heralded the end of Tom's over and he light-heartedly set off for his patch on the mid-wicket boundary, well pleased with himself. Peter Jackson waved a gigantic keeper's glove at Tarry who responded with a nod of thanks. It was going Little Dow's way. But where was the Slogger Stevenson the East End lads knew? Well, he had to open up soon didn't he? And he did.

CREEK CRICKET CLUB AFTER TWO EXCELLENT OVERS

Stevenson	*not out*	*0*
Peters	*not out*	*0*
extras		*1*
TOTAL		*1 without loss*

Trevor White returned, having peeled off some of his clothing, as no doubt his wife had done by now. He was to resume at the pavilion end. Lily Grace was silent, because her lavender water and talc said everything . . . loudly.

Slogger's patience had run out; he pulled back his shoulders, arched his back and sent the first ball of the over back from where it came, but four or five times higher. A magnificent six and a splendid way to get off the mark. Seated villagers scattered as the ball re-entered the village's atmosphere and clumped against the green and cream weather boarding of the front of the pavilion. Aubrey Padgett dutifully waited for Lily's signal, suspender belt showing, arms held aloft, before marking the runs against Slogger's name. Molly the labrador thought it was all good fun and set off to retrieve the ball, sniffing around in the long grass beside the pavilion until she came across the correct scent, finally sinking her teeth into the carefully polished leather. The irate Creek on-lookers and villagers chased and cursed Molly who, had she been of the opposite sex, would have undergone a most unfortunate experience usually executed by a vet.

'Get that bleedin' ball out your north and south!' demanded Vince Clayton, but the labrador never answered, probably owing to the fact that her north and south was filled with a cricket ball.

'We must get that ball back. Does anybody know anything about dogs?' asked an anxious Mrs Robbins.

'Not me,' replied Pumps.

'All I know is that you never kick a dog in the balls when you've got your hand in his mouth,' muttered Julian Jannik.

There were giggles a-plenty as villagers set off to round up the fun-loving beast. The incident didn't have the disruptive scope of the well-endowed female who had graced Twickenham and the living-rooms of a few million TV viewers, displaying her attributes, but it was worrying all the same to Jackson, who until then thought his side had the upper hand. Julian, bemused by the concern, knew only too well that if they left the dog alone it would get bored and drop the ball. He set off for a quick chat with the other Molly some forty yards or so along the boundary rope.

'Poor dog, it's only enjoying itself,' he said to her, pecking her lightly on the cheek without checking whether or not her parents were scrutinising the action.

'Yeah, next they'll be drawing a whip on her,' pondered Molly.

'Gorblimey, girl, I'm getting all excited again, don't say things like that when I've got a game of Jiminy Cricket to be getting on with.'

'Oh dear, I suppose you like black stockings too, eh?'

'Not really, darling, they don't show up on me.'

The two laughed their heads off, Julian offered another peck and returned to his team-mates.

'All right there, my son?' asked Winston.

'No you ain't, she's mine,' quipped the jovial Julian.

Back at the wicket Trevor White was low, six runs off him and a soggy ball in return. He studied the teethmarks as the guilty animal was dispatched to the canine equivalent of an early bath. How quickly Trevor's spirits rose and fell; an excellent first over and then . . . just because he'd been clouted for six on the long hop and had his ball chewed. At that wretched moment he felt like he'd come third in a game of chess or got an inflatable woman pregnant.

Lily Grace studied the ball with Trevor and Jackson; it now resembled a pin cushion.

'Shit! Look at that,' demanded the bowler.

'Language!' yelped Lily Grace. Molly the labrador yelped too as her master clouted her rump with the nasty end of her lead.

It was decided to play on with the same ball. A half a dozen more overs and then it would be tea, and the bitten lump would merely be a fine conversation piece.

After much delay, Trevor bowled to Slogger from the pavilion end.

A few spots of rain fell on Slogger's forehead as he faced up to Trevor with an oddly retaken guard of off stump. The squarer stance enabled him to get behind the ball more quickly to execute his favourite stroke over deep mid-on. If he missed it was LBW, but after such a slow start he felt like taking the chance. Jackson realised his ploy and moved Baird across from the front of the pavilion to the on side, some twenty feet in from the boundary, within whispering distance of John Copeland. A dangerous proximity because the pair hadn't spoken since John's retriever had bagged a pheasant Baird's shotgun had taken on the rise.

A snicked four between Smythe and Baker B. saw Slogger comfortably into double figures and the score moved merrily along without incident until Eddie Peters was clean bowled by a top-class yorker from the jubilant harmonium-mender for 8.

A rumble in the sky over Berkshire was heard in Little Dow and fielders called for long-sleeved sweaters. There were only six to go round and the cricketers nearest to the pavilion got them. Luckily, Joe Robbins was one of them, for he had shivered to the point of sea-sickness. Anglers on the river's edge erected their bright-green umbrellas and hoped the ensuing downpour would oxygenate the fish into action.

The rain began to fall and Geoffrey Baird's tinted specs took on a mottled look, and exactly an hour and a quarter into the Creek Cricket Club's innings the umpires, after short deliberation, called the players in for an early tea. At least there was blue sky in the distance as the players sprinted for shelter.

A hundred or so folk crammed into the pavilion, a far greater number than had ever graced a village hall function, and Aubrey Padgett was heard to lament for the type of covers seen in a washed-out Test match transmission. The players gathered around him to study the situation. It was far too early to boast the upper hand, so Peter and Winston spoke inanely of the day in general, the office junior preferring to do most of the listening.

CREEK CRICKET CLUB AT THE TEA INTERVAL

Stevenson	*not out*		*19*
Peters		*b White*	*8*
Clayton	*not out*		*1*
extras			*2*
TOTAL			*30 for 1 wicket*

Mrs Robbins, invigorated by her husband's unexpected

knock earlier, and her voluntary assistant Alice, lined out the home-made buttered scones in two long lines, resembling blazered Test sides during presentation to royalty. Mounds of egg and cucumber sandwiches appeared as though by magic. Julian Jannik was nowhere to be seen.

The players, worn out by the fifty-yard dash in the rain, wandered into the tea room at a leisurely pace, laughing exaggeratedly at banal comments, the way that studious part-time cricketers do. Comments about straight bats, true wickets and near perfect atmospheric conditions flew hither and thither. Molly, the dog in the doghouse, sprawled out on all-fours in everybody's way, while Julian was preparing himself and his good lady for the same sort of stance.

The sandwiches seemed to have mislaid their crusts, looking painfully thin in mountainous bundles, bearing no relation to the bread-doorstep and cheese-wedge variety of the anglers downstream. In the pavilion sounds of spike on floorboard obliterated the unfriendly roar of the summer rainstorm; ligament oil and lavender water cancelled out the delightful fragrance of watered grass and flora. The whole façade took on the semblance of a wedding reception, with the guests taking up to six or seven sandwiches at a time and then swallowing them without chewing. Curious eyes stared at the remaining crumbs for a hint of the filling — tuna fish or sardine, pressed ham or luncheon meat? To be in the dry was all that mattered.

Little Dow would have been a fine spot for fishermen had it not been for the plaintive cries of LBW appealers or excited spectators, and many a patient Izaak Walton had concealed himself in the reeds. Rudi Waites for one merely relieved himself in the reeds. He had developed a great desire to slam a six yards over mid wicket, landing the ball in the Thames with a dull kind of splash reminiscent of a returning space probe plopping into the ocean. That would have pleased the descendants of Izaak no end, of course. Knowing Rudi's luck he would have hit a passing rented cruiser, travelling west on a marine holiday full of boisterous day- and ego-tripping people, doomed to bubble down to the riverbed, never to be seen or heard again. Rudi had the power to effect such a desire, and should Lord Smythe in the final over bowl him one of his dollies there was every possibility he would.

Rudi, the young powerhouse (as opposed to Julian, who was by now a young pumping station), chatted incessantly to the villagers, occasionally in the *patois* of Barbados, but more often than not in his native Cockney tongue. They were warming to him, even though they'd seen very few, if any, blacks in the village. Of course they were well aware that black people made excellent cricketers, recalling what a fine, upstanding gentleman the celebrated Sir Gary Sobers was, but there was still trepidation from villagers who should have known better than to trepidate.

Compliments to the chef screamed loudly and haughtily from all directions, and Mrs Robbins smiled smiles of contentment and gratitude. Alice kept her head down and poured the teas. She neither expected nor received any kind of compliment.

Suddenly, the first hand disturbed the geometric beauty of the sandwich display, causing the floodgates of thrusting hands to open. Plates rattled and both East End and middle-class manners disappeared beneath the piles of sandwiches. Philip Trevelyan asked Montgomery Holt if he recalled the six magnificent catches the late Wally Grout of Australia took at the Headingley Test.

'Who the hell was Wally Grout, man, if you don't mind me asking like?' Monty asked, very much in the dark.

'No, I don't mind at all,' Trevelyan went on, 'Wally Grout, the late Wally Grout I am sorry to say, was Australia's finest wicket-keeper. Played for Queensland if I remember rightly, or perhaps it was New South Wales. Anyway it was one of those settlements over there. Tell you what, old boy, you reminded me of him in a strange sort of way, you know.'

'How strange a way?' Monty asked.

'Oh, not too strange, he never wore claret and blue keeper's pads for a start. But he was agile, like you, and don't forget he stood up to some of the fastest bowlers of all time.'

Monty, who knew a little of the game's history, but not too much, interrupted the storyteller. 'I thought Lillee and Thomson were the greatest Australian bowlers of all time.'

'Lillee and Thomson, good lord man, Richie Benaud bowled faster than them. Brave man was Wally, and a darn good chap by all accounts too. Bloody sight more acceptable than that brash chap of recent years . . . er . . . oh, what's his name? Rodney Marsh,' the worldly-wise Trevelyan complained.

'Yeah well, he started going downhill when he started playing for them Tampax Bay Rowdies. He was great when he was at Loftus Road,' replied Monty.

'Loftus Road, eh. Is that a street near where you chaps come from? Well, I never did . . . um . . . interesting.'

The conversation had become well and truly exhausted, each participant unaware of the other's profound ignorance. They sipped at their lukewarm tea and parted company. Monty went in search of a cigarette, while Trevelyan discussed the merits and similarities of Keith Miller and Ian Botham to Mrs Robbins as she emptied the dregs of another teapot down the home team's wash-basin.

The sandwiches had been gobbled and the tea had been drunk. If the game had been played in the East End of London, the punch would have been drunk and drunks would have been punched! A few crumbs remained on the china plates and the players assembled outside the pavilion on the wet grass. Blue sky was upon them, and it promised to be a delightful evening session.

Parry Taylor knew Lord Smutsy would be late, so

without labouring the point he held back as best he could in the hope that The Important Man would soon be along. Some children who were playing a make-believe Test match in the outfield with a sensible tennis ball were ushered away by Lily Grace. They left to an occasional raspberry, though none would dare admit to the deed. Sunshine broke through and jewels of rain glistened across the meadow, the trees swayed no more and all fell silent until the gentle purr of Lord Smythe's Range Rover was heard approaching.

The members of the Creek Cricket Club appreciated the slack way of life the Little Dow folk enjoyed. By now they would be sweating blood and fighting four deep for a cardboard-flavoured hamburger if they were back in the Ilford High Road or a similar venue. No, this was the life, albeit a brief part. The world of good manners, crustless sandwiches, cold beer and sunshine beamed down upon them and was readily accepted by all — bar one.

Julian Jannik had disappeared beneath an adjacent broad bean field, beyond the allotments, there to lay with Molly Martin. His broad shoulders sheltered the tender areas of her body from the rays of sunshine. She marvelled at his athleticism, adored the way he played cricket and dreamed of the way he made love.

He got up only the once, to relieve himself at the pavilion end. It was a delivery of excellent line and length.

— FOUR —

The Final Session

Parry and Lily walked out first, hands in pockets, not speaking, like Dickie Bird and David Constant would have done. Not because they weren't friends; it was just that Parry could think of nothing to say to his female counterpart. He questioned her knowledge of the finer points of the game so he chose to limp out to the wicket in silence. Madam Grace strode out with the purpose of a guest speaker pounding down the aisle at a Women's Institute gathering.

Peter Jackson, padded up, strolled behind, delighted to be basking in the evening sunshine. His shadow stretched long and thin across the outfield. He was followed by eight white floppy hats, a couple of sleeveless sweaters, Geoffrey Baird plus specs, and the balding Joe Robbins. Not until the fielders were stationed at their rightful places did the Creek batsmen consider leaving their team on the boundary ropes. As the two openers set off for their respective creases a smattering of applause echoed across the meadow, causing the grateful but surprised brace of batsmen to look back. Slogger Stevenson was undefeated on 19, Vince Clayton was just off the mark with a neatly taken single from the last over before the tea session.

'Man in!' shrieked Jackson inaccurately, for there were two of them and neither were new batsmen, but the fielders clapped all the same.

Slogger's distinctive yellow cords beamed out as luminous as a field of rapeseed on a dull evening. There were looks of grim determination on the openers' faces as the humour drained away with the seriousness of the job in hand — though Alfie Donald was keeping the lower-order batsmen well amused with his characteristic one-liners.

'Have you ever slept with a homosexual?' he asked Pumps Parker teasingly.

'No, but I've slept with a bloke who has,' said Pumps with gay abandon, having had the gag thrust upon him at many a cricket game and club disco.

Clayton was to receive the first ball of the new session and he was busy taking middle and leg guard as Lord Smythe, the decadent second slip, ploughed through the grass to take up his sacred role.

Lady Smythe had a gigantic rear end and played croquet badly but with great authority. She pretended to be young and attractive but the years had been unkind to her immense lower frame. Like his lordship, she knew very little about cricket, and proved it by standing ten yards in from the ropes, her camera hanging limply like a general's binoculars. She was eager to obtain a snap of her husband in action in the slips and was quite oblivious to the muted giggles of the boundary-hugging on-lookers. Barnaby Baker took on the brave role of bringing the embarrassing tidings of Lady Smythe's trespass to her husband, who was already crouching with enthusiastic, ungainly poise. He looked around and signalled to her as if he were a bookie's runner at Newmarket. She failed to comprehend the manic gestures of her waving husband and turned around to glance at the Range Rover perched behind her. Perhaps he had forgotten to apply the handbrake? No . . . all was well with the Smythe-mobile . . . Ah, could it be that Smutsy was in need of a sweater? Yes, that was it, a long-sleeved sweater was required.

'What colour?' she bellowed.

'Do what?' replied the confused landowner.

'What colour do you want?' she repeated.

'Oh, just hoppit, there's a love,' he yelled, turning his back on the whole embarrassing affair.

'Oh, I suppose any jumper will do so long as it's warm. Reggie must be feeling the breeze a little,' she thought to herself as she mounted the Range Rover.

Trevor White was about to bowl. He shuffled his feet, leaned forward as before and some three or four yards from the stumps the revving of a huge engine brought him to an abrupt halt.

'Jesus Christ, I don't believe this,' he moaned.

Clayton raised his hand, in case Trevor White was intending to go through with the delivery despite the mayhem. Dogs' ears pricked up nervously, and heads turned as if following a torpedo-like first service at Wimbledon. Crouching players relaxed their positions and stared towards the disruption. Lady Smythe noticed nothing as she threw the steering wheel into full lock in a most masculine manner, veering away from the boundary in a largish arc towards the white concrete lions that guarded the gates to the estate.

'What on earth's the woman doing?' begged Lord Smutsy.

'Search me,' said Philip Trevelyan.

'I'm dreadfully sorry about this, chaps,' Smutsy continued apologetically. 'Can't get the staff, you know. Right then, as you were.'

Down he crouched. Down Jackson crouched also, only too pleased he hadn't had to get involved with the defusing of an awkward incident.

'What a bloody woman,' whispered the red-faced Smythe.

'What a silly cow,' muttered Trevor White as he strolled back to his white metal marker after the false start, annoyed at the unnecessary expenditure of energy.

'What a wanker,' thought Vince Clayton to himself as he glanced at the crouching aristocrat.

The exhaust had risen far into the sky to join the less obtrusive wisps of light cloud that passed towards Oxford on tip-toe. The mechanical purring of perfection had more or less disappeared beyond the giant wrought-iron barriers before Trevor dared attempt another charge. Clayton tapped at the crease lightly as though nothing much had happened.

The bowler clutched the ball with a finger each side of the seam. He had carefully polished it on one side, hoping for a little turn in the air as it shot towards the receiver, but it was hardly likely, such movements being restricted to overcast days and magnificent bowling. Trevor was a good but not brilliant graduate of the swing bowler's academy. Funny how Ian Botham in only a few years of first-class cricket had popularised the swinging ball in village cricket. Trevor polished the ball on the one side and hoped for miracles equal to those Botham had performed. It was hardly likely, as Trevor White couldn't manage three Shredded Wheats like his hero.

Clayton played the first three deliveries of the final session with ease, defiantly sending the ball back to the bowler on two of the occasions and sending Trevelyan sprawling with the third.

'Well fielded!' called Jackson to the man with the green-stained knee-caps.

Then came one of Clayton's splendid strokes that looked four all the way. It headed towards Joe Robbins at deep fine leg who stood in its path and somehow stopped what seemed a certain boundary. The old man was having quite a game in what many hoped would be his final season for Little Dow. The effort had stung fingers and shin alike, but at least it was only two runs not four.

Mrs Robbins nearly had a seizure seeing her poor husband wringing his hands and bouncing on one leg. She sprinted to the ropes with a handful of lint and a bottle of TCP, awaiting permission to take the field like a football trainer at a top level match. Joe noticed her concern and felt silly. He stuck his stinging hand into his pocket and turned his back on his wife. He dreaded her being compared to Lady Smythe. Mrs Robbins reluctantly returned to the pavilion where she related to Alice all the many injuries and illnesses her Joe had sustained during their many years of blissful marriage (though she chose to omit the dreadful dose of the crabs he contracted during National Service in Aden . . . perhaps she had never found out about that).

Clayton took a single with a gentle push wide of mid-off from the last ball of the over, anxious to get the score moving along. He winked at Lily Grace as he arrived at the other end, causing her to shuffle her flat-heeled tie-ups with embarrassment. She was flattered despite the feeling of impertinence and she eyed the young rascal up and down as he adjusted his box after the sprint. Meanwhile, Trevor White replaced his sweater and wiped the sweat from his brow. Not a bad over, but Trevor White had been known to bowl better.

Slogger hadn't received a ball since tea and strode up the wicket to remind Clayton of that fact. He shrugged his shoulders and the pair returned to their respective positions.

Tom Tarry's bowling was accurate but hardly penetrating. Jackson needed to change the bowling before the two hard-hitters got their eye in. Tarry looked a little disappointed, but the captain barely noticed as he gave instructions to Nicholas O'Connor, the replacement bowler.

With the solitary loss of Eddie Peters, Creek Cricket

Club had mustered 32 runs, leaving 121 runs to win with nine wickets standing. Rudi and Winston were still to bat, both capable of a century if they weren't too hungover. Things were not particularly rosy in the meadow for the home side.

Nicholas O'Connor had been a good servant to Little Dow, although he said little at club meetings at the Plough Hotel. He was a man of few words, though he felt strongly about female umpires and yellow cricket flannels. His own whites were a size too large, and at the ripe old age of forty there was little chance he would ever grow into them.

Vince Clayton patted the crease and chatted to Slogger Stevenson as Jackson arranged his field. Whether it was strategic banter or a dirty joke was hard to say, but Slogger knew many blue stories, and little about strategy. Clayton had donned a white floppy hat to celebrate the arrival of the evening sun. It looked like whipped cream on a Black Forest gâteau as it nonchalantly lay on the head of the magnificent athlete. He wasn't as massive as Clive Lloyd, the celebrated West Indian captain, but many of his strokes resembled those of the great man, especially his lofty lobs over the bowler's head. Clayton screwed up his eyes to focus on the in-coming O'Connor, patting the crease in unison with the bowler's footsteps. O'Connor bowled a stray delivery, and Clayton sent it screaming through the covers for three quickly sprinted runs.

'Stay!' ordered Clayton.

'Fair enough, my son,' responded Slogger, who was beginning to tire.

He preferred to build up his score with fours and sixes and hadn't run so much since he was caught chatting up someone else's date at the cricket club disco earlier that season. Clayton moved on to seven not out and leaned on the handle of his bat as some field adjustments took place. Philip Trevelyan moved into a deep gully position and Lord Smythe and Baker B. were moved closer together, releasing third man to fill the gap on the off side.

Nicholas O'Connor jogged in lazily, licking his fingers in the process, and released a fine delivery, even if it was a fraction short. There was a blur of yellow as Slogger took two steps up the wicket and smashed the ball into the sky. Exactly the same destination as his first six, the ball cracked against the weather boarding of the changing rooms and another half dozen were signalled by the arm-stretching umpire.

The Creek players cheered and whooped at the stroke as Slogger returned to his crease, more than delighted with his excursion up the strip. The polite crowd applauded the shot vigorously, rarely having seen the same batsman strike two sixes in the same innings. The frenzied attacker swept some dangling strands of hair from his eyes and settled down to the third ball of the over. A couple of white cabbage butterflies fluttered by, causing the man to ease the proceedings for a second. They flew on without apology, settling on the brick face of Lord Smythe's wall to watch the rest of the game in far more suitable attire than Slogger Stevenson.

O'Connor tried round the wicket, Slogger tried the same smash. Eyes shot into the air tracing the trajectory of the leather missile.

'Owzat!' screamed Jackson behind the stumps.

The slip fielders raised their hands, though none had really heard the snick, and Slogger Stevenson was dismissed, caught behind.

'Did I touch that?' asked the victim to the catcher.

'Afraid so, old boy,' endorsed Jackson.

'Oh shit!' exclaimed the disappointed batsman. 'I didn't mean to,'

'Good knock though, my friend,' consoled the keeper.

Slogger didn't respond to the compliment, because he was far too busy excusing himself from the fray. Jackson was right: Slogger had made contact with the ball, but it had also been a splendid knock — just what one would have expected from Colin Milburn at his mightiest, way back in 1968. Milburn was once cautioned by the upstanding Tom Graveney after a good knock in the First Test against Pakistan in 1967 when Graveney accused the man of playing for himself and the crowd, saddened by the disregard for the other batsmen. Colin Milburn had sacrificed his wicket that day, and Slogger Stevenson had done very much the same thing at Little Dow. The difference was that Slogger had set Creek well on their way with his adventurous style, and his captain, Winston Waites, was absolutely delighted.

Slogger raised his bat as he crossed the boundary ropes, acknowledging the rich applause of the appreciative crowd.

'How many did I get, man?' asked Stevenson.

'Quite a few, hang on,' said Winston trotting across to the scorer. 'Excuse me, how many did Slogger score?' Aubrey Padgett smiled and studied the book before him.

'Let me see now, Stevenson S. caught Peter Jackson, bowled Nicholas O'Connor for 25. Should have been more, threw his wicket away . . . the silly lad.'

'Yes OK, thank you very much,' retorted Waites, then shouted across to his de-padding mate.

'You got twenty-five, Slogger. Not bad, eh?'

'Should have been more, Win, the wicket's slow and the bowling ain't that great. Should have been a lot more. Who's in next?'

'Screwball Pinder.'

Screwball Pinder walked in with little sense of purpose, a fag hanging from the corner of his mouth, leaving his team-mates to wonder why he was always so high in the batting order. Truth of the matter was that he drove the mini-bus to away matches and insisted on a rest between batting and driving, and although it had been an entourage of private cars this time because of the unreliability of the bus over such a long journey, he had been placed at number 4 by Winston's force of habit. Ten yards in from the boundary he returned in search of a bat. He probably felt he could play just as well without one, and he probably could have.

Screwball took an unexpected single, securing one of his best-ever personal scores, before being bowled middle stump the next over by Trevor White. He searched for his dog-end as he returned to the pavilion, but there was no sign of smoke because it had been well stubbed. He would have to light another.

'Perhaps a fraction longer would have been a good thing?' asked Winston.

'Piss off!' Screwball requested, with little regard for the young schoolboys who waited for his autograph. Rudi Waites was in next and the fielding side looked visibly concerned as the hugely-built lad ambled confidently up to the wicket.

'Man in,' said the keeper.

The players applauded his arrival, hoping he was going to be a reincarnation of the late Screwball Pinder. The fielders subconsciously took a step back, while Lord Smythe spat on his hands for no apparent reason. Rudi was a better batsman than Trevor a bowler, and it would be an interesting confrontation. Winston watched his brother take guard, then glanced once more at the scoreboard. There was still an awful lot to do.

Stevenson	*ct Jackson*	*b O'Connor*	*25*
Peters		*b White*	*8*
Clayton	*not out*		*7*
Pinder		*b White*	*1*
Waites R.	*not out*		*0*
extras			*2*
TOTAL			*43 for 3 wickets*

Rudi looked around the boundary, mentally choosing the sitings of his glorious strokes. He was itching to put one through the windscreen of Lord Smythe's Range Rover, and there was every chance he would do as it rested a few feet beyond deep mid-wicket. White was to bowl to Waites R., there were seven wickets remaining and 110 runs were needed to win.

Lady Smythe had freewheeled the Rover down the arched drive from the grand house owned by the second slip. Disturbed gravel and broadside breeze were the only sound. Her head-scarf was wrapped tightly around her head, despite the charming burst of sunshine, covering her richly-perfumed hair beneath the silk-screened design. The knot rested uncomfortably on the dimple of her chin, an inch or so from her bottom lip, similar to the strap of a member of the Household Cavalry. She had whistled a few bars of Haydn before turning the key to start the engine, drowning the works of the great composer and the sound of crushed gravel alike, and had turned into the meadow with little due care or attention. It was her Reggie's land, so her privilege to do (or not do) so. She parked the car far too close to the outfield, the front wheels on the boundary's edge.

Jackson had finally arranged his field to face Rudi, but Lord Smythe was still in the slips. Hardly surprising for he couldn't run, and preferred to save his energy for the final over of the day, his rent for the use of his field. He had also given Aubrey Padgett the day off to score. A kind and considerate man was Lord Smythe.

Lily Grace shot out her arm and Trevor's run was halted in full cry.

'Just a moment,' begged the umpire, 'there appears to be an intruder.'

And she was right. All eyes stared across to the boundary from where her ladyship was stamping across the grass with a beige, chunky-knit jumper across one arm like a dead sheep. The fielders relaxed and Rudi slammed the wicket in frustration. His concentration had been broken.

'There you are, and next time bring it with you when you come,' moaned Lady Smythe in headmistress fashion. She then espied Peter Jackson behind the wicket.

'Ah, Peter, how are you? And how's Joan?'

Peter answered 'Fine' to both questions with embarrassed haste.

'You really must come over to dinner very soon. Pheasants are rising any day, you simply must come for the first roast.'

'We'd . . . um . . . love to. Thank you.'

'What's this then?' asked Lord Smutsy.

'It's the jumper you asked for. Now put it on before you catch your death of cold.'

'My dear, I never asked for any such thing, and besides it's not even white.'

'For fuck's sake, what the bleedin' hell's going on 'ere?' asked the infuriated Rudi Waites.

'I beg your pardon, young man,' demanded Lady Smythe.

'We are trying to play cricket here, darling, why don't you hop it, eh?' he replied with little temper remaining.

'Yes, clear off, my dear, otherwise I'm going to lose my head in front of all these fine sportsmen,' warned her husband.

His demands were never questioned, regardless of whom they were intended to hurt. Lady Smythe knew this only too well, turning on her heels to walk briskly back to the car, as deflated as a star batsman uprooted first ball. Titterings swelled around the ropes but nobody dared admit to their giggles for fear of future reprisals. No shoulder heaved up and down, but the titterings were there all the same.

'And leave the damned Range Rover exactly where it is,' yelled the Lord in her wake.

It was a shrewd afterthought, for it was quite a walk back to the manor, and all uphill too, a most unfriendly gradient for one who had tired oneself with the bowling of the final six deliveries. Lady Smythe leaned forward to negotiate the same slanted gravel path. She was in a wretched mood. She said nothing, not even out of earshot, and hoped there would be no outburst while they were entertaining at dinner later that evening. If only he would take a wicket, *that* would dilute the whole affair.

Trevor White to Rudi Waites, in conditions now ideal for cricket.

Trevor bowled a deliberately short ball to the new batsman, hoping he would edge it to the slips or behind. Rudi was far too experienced to play such a stroke and knowing it would be that sort of delivery, he swivelled around and stroked it to the on-side boundary, just as he had seen Viv Richards do on television. The ball came to rest somewhere between the aforementioned chub tempter at the river's edge and the long riverbank reeds where Julian first felt Molly's firmness. A fabulous stroke indeed . . . as was Rudi's boundary! He was off the mark and he and Clayton seemed a formidable force against the questionable skills of the Little Dow side.

The ensuing quarter of an hour was sheer delight as Clayton and Rudi pasted the tame attack around the meadow. Oak trees and pavilion walls trembled as they met the full force of the batsmen's boundaries. There had to be a change of bowling if Little Dow were to secure a result — either that or a freak thunderstorm — and both Nicholas O'Connor and Trevor White were rested despite the harmonium-mender's two wickets. Tom Tarry was to take the next over at the oak-tree end, while Geoffrey Baird, the objectionable Geoffrey Baird, would resume at the pavilion end in place of Trevor White. White had played himself into the ground at the same time his wife had played herself *on* to the ground. Tom Tarry hardly looked strong enough to bowl six balls, one after the other, but he gritted his teeth with utter determination as he rubbed the ball and sent the whole field a yard or two further back. Tarry was absolutely right, the way to trap Rudi was having him caught deep in the outfield, but for the moment he satisfied himself and his captain with a prized maiden. It was a notable achievement against two fine batsmen who were seeing the ball with ease.

Geoffrey Baird's first ball was a no-ball in every sense. Over-accentuating the grip. As though he were Ken Mackay or similar, his foot stepped over the bowler's crease and the delivery bounced twice before reaching the other end. Vince Clayton, laughing loudly, lost the golden opportunity of cracking another boundary through his lack of concentration. Clayton took a mere two runs off the over and glanced towards the sky, wondering how long his side had to reach the required number of runs.

In the next over Tarry trapped Rudi leg-before with a crafty ball that turned in off the wicket. The decision was plumb and Rudi did not question Parry Taylor's word. Rudi had added eighteen runs to the score and Little Dow were grateful that it wasn't more. It should have been, Rudi being by far the best cricketer on show. Winston replaced his brother at the crease.

'Would you like guard?' asked Parry politely.

'Two please,' replied Winston.

Parry was delighted to converse with somebody who knew a little about the game, recalling how, when he asked Screwball Pinder if he required a guard, the lad had told him not to bother as he had just put one out.

Tom Tarry had taken his first wicket at club level and was keen to search for his second. Winston observed the field placements for a while before taking up his squarish stance. Parry Taylor bowed his head towards the bowler's crease as Tom Tarry hopped in. Winston prodded and missed, then looked towards the heavens for accurate inspiration.

'That was a close one,' said Julian Jannik to Molly Martin.

Their lips met for the umpteenth time that day as a hand slid up and down the white trouser leg . . . as Tom Tarry rubbed the ball in preparation for his next delivery. The crowd had swelled as staff from the joint general store and post office (the entire shopping complex at Little Dow) gathered around Aubrey Padgett to ascertain match proceedings while they had been selling bread, bacon rashers and postal orders.

Winston arched his back like a golfer as the ball spun towards him off the seam. He sent the ball blistering along the lush green carpet, through the shadows. Four runs all the way — all the way, that is, until John Copeland sprinted across to cut off the shot. Winston hadn't even bothered to run, certain it was four. Everybody clapped John's excellent pick-up and his nifty return to Jackson's gloves. Copeland rarely did things like that, so he enjoyed it thoroughly. Winston was still to get off the mark.

'Unlucky, Winston, good stroke that,' whispered Jackson to his office junior.

'Thanks, Mr Jackson, good fielding though.'

The wicket keeper crouched and Winston prodded as Tarry came in to continue an over that came to be one of the talking topics in the village for many a day.

A good ball from Tarry, accurate in both line and length, scuttled towards Winston's bat. He played across the line and the ball went through to the wicket-keeper. Jackson threw the ball into the air, yelled 'Howzat!' and surprised close fielders loyally followed suit. Parry Taylor was completely unimpressed, ignoring the appeal and taking the weight off his false leg.

'That was out!' shouted Lily Grace at square leg.

'Do what?' asked the disbelieving Winston Waites.

'That can't be out, man. Winston ain't got no runs yet. He'll be bleedin' livid,' warned Vince Clayton.

'That was OUT,' yelled Grace with authority.

'Silly old crab, you want your bleedin' brown bread examined if you ask me.'

'She's given you out, Winston,' reminded the wicket-keeper.

'Oh, come on now, Mr Jackson, you know bloody well

that was never out in a bleedin' month of Sundays. I never touched the fucking ball.'

'Best be on your way, Winston old man. It's not cricket to argue, you know,' his boss reminded him. Winston strolled across to Parry Taylor, who hadn't signalled out, nor had he heard the snick.

'Was that out, sir?' asked Winston politely.

'If the other umpire heard the thin edge, then I'm afraid it was caught behind. I didn't hear it myself, but that's why there are two umpires, to ensure fair play.'

'Fair play? FAIR PLAY?' choked the victim. 'You've got to be bleedin' joking, mate.'

Winston turned and stormed back towards the pavilion to the backdrop of a few youths who slow hand-clapped him en route. Most of the spectators didn't really know what to think. A similar thing had happened to David Gower in a Test Match at Old Trafford against the Pakistanis. He had stood his ground and was adjudged to be not out. Perhaps Winston should have ignored his boss and done likewise. Once he had walked the decision could not be reversed.

'Unlucky, me old china,' said Clayton, who strolled a few paces with Winston before changing course and heading towards Lily Grace.

'Come off it, darling, that wasn't out. We never heard nothing up the other end.'

'Well, I did. And I'd be pleased if you would refrain from calling me darling too, young man. It makes me sound like a gangster's moll,' warned the woman whose very glare could have sent the Krays into submission.

'Don't worry, man,' said Rudi comfortingly as the two met a few yards from the boundary. Winston was livid. He threw his bat at the kit-bag from a good ten yards, causing the gaggle of worried mothers to gather in their youngsters, safe from the rantings of the distraught youth.

Stevie Whiteman was the next man in.

Stevenson	*ct Jackson*	*b O'Connor*	*25*
Peters		*b White*	*8*
Clayton	*not out*		*21*
Pinder		*b White*	*1*
Waites R.	*LBW*	*b Tarry*	*18*
Waites W.	*ct Jackson*	*b Tarry*	*0*
extras			*4*
TOTAL			*77 for 5 wickets*

'To this day, I cannot say what came over me regarding that Winston Waites affair. He certainly never touched the ball, and, as wicket-keeper, I was certainly the nearest to the man at the time. I knew he was a damn good batsman, so the appeal was worthwhile on that score. But I must say here and now that it was a most unsporting thing to do, and was certainly not cricket. I understand Winston's remorse, especially being caught by his boss, an ironic quirk that did little to defuse the embarrassing situation.

Lily Grace knew as much about cricket as I did about the East End of London. I felt and still feel wretched regarding the whole sordid affair, and desperately wish I hadn't bothered with what was no more than a cheap confidence trick aimed at the umpire. Sorry, Winston old man, completely my fault . . . don't tell the chaps at work, eh? That wouldn't be cricket either.'

Stevie Whiteman wasn't a great cricketer but he adored the game nevertheless. He walked to the crease ignorant of the fracas, his nerves as cool as they ever were. He did all the right things during his entry and the wrong things during his innings. He looked at the sky, squinted his eyes, and rolled his arm around like Botham. He had made a few runs but suffered from asthma and inconsistency. His highest score had been against the East London Police XI two days after he'd been done for drinking and driving. The three-month ban had injected venom into the mediocre batsman, enticing him to take his revenge of the local constabulary for the best part of two hours, culminating in a career best 78.

Whiteman had been weaned into the game by his pen-pushing father who, although British through and through, had worshipped the ground Sir Garfield Sobers trod. A rather fitting paradox that Sobers played his first match for the West Indies at the same age as Stevie made his debut for Creek Cricket Club, seventeen. They were both orthodox slow left-arm bowlers, until the West Indian, over the years, fancied the runs more than the wickets, and his captain at that time, Frank Worrell, had changed his pace to fast-medium for tactical reasons. Stevie Whiteman as an orthodox left armer was waywardly unorthodox, so there the similarities ended, except neither had much chance of playing for England. Batting was a completely different matter. While Sobers had that innate desire to attack, his batting was always controlled and powerful. Whiteman's was *un*controlled and powerful, the batting style resembling Bob Willis or Brian Statham.

After a few words with Vince Clayton, who was looking good on an unbeaten 21, Stevie purposefully took a middle and leg guard before staring around at the field placements.

It is said that Mike Brearley refused to watch the lengthy run-up of a fast bowler for fear of being mesmerised. He chose to hum instead to help cool his nerves, his favourite piece being a cello passage from the Razumovsky Quartets. Whiteman was the same, except that he didn't really care to watch the delivery either. With the few steps of Tom Tarry, Stevie had time only for the first two bars of 'I'm Forever Blowing Bubbles' before smashing his first ball for his first boundary. He was off the mark, end of the over, ripples of applause for Tarry's fine effort, and Creek needed 72 to win.

The sun was sinking with the burdens of a changeable

day, and the shadows stretched long across the outfield. Geoffrey Baird's shadow shot away like a darkened highway, from mid-on to forward short leg. He looked set for the man of the match award and that delighted nobody. In a perverse way, Jackson willed Clayton on towards his century and Tom Tarry on towards his hat-trick, the simultaneous desires impossible to achieve.

O'Connor was back on the attack, and it was to be the first major tactical error of the match. The bowler may very well have physically resembled Derek Underwood, but he lacked the Kent man's stamina and accuracy over a long spell.

Parry Taylor and his female counterpart had met to discuss stumps between Tarry and O'Connor's overs. The light wasn't bad yet, but it was getting darker by the minute.

'What do you think?' asked Parry.

'Not sure, old chap, what do you think?' replied Lily, unsure what he was talking about. Perhaps he was asking about the game in general, perhaps he was talking about something intimate behind the pavilion — she had no idea. Parry Taylor's clue in this mid-wicket charade was a glance towards the sky, but Lily hadn't noticed. Parry longed for a light meter, and Lily longed for a letter from her niece away at boarding school.

Peter Jackson walked from his wicket-keeping position to join the consulting adults. He knew exactly what the discussion was about. Meanwhile, Julian and Molly, who weren't keen on the daylight anyway, yearned for the dark blue anonymity of the night.

Winston Waites was sulking and Rudi Waites was smoking a joint, so Vince Clayton chose to represent the visiting side during the discussion.

'How many more overs then?' Parry asked the others.

'Yes, how many more overs?' seconded Lily Grace. The discussion developed to include other participants in the proximity. What did Vince Clayton think, and what about

Lord Smutsy Smythe? After all it was his pitch, and perhaps there was a certain time when he wanted it back.

'How about ten more overs then?' suggested Jackson after studying the score.

'Sounds good to me, ten overs then?' said Lily.

'Ten overs everybody,' yelled Parry Taylor.

'I fear it will be considerably less than ten overs for me,' muttered Stevie Whiteman.

Pumps Parker and Eddie Peters confronted the scorer's table, keen to know exactly how many runs were needed from each of the final overs. Aubrey scratched his head, mumbled a few numbers then spoke.

'Creek Cricket Club require 7.2 runs per over for victory. Little Dow require 5 wickets.'

The rate was passed around the spectators until everybody but Julian Jannik and Molly Martin knew of it.

Clayton smacked a spectacular raspberry lolly through the covers for four off the first of O'Connor's next over, and went on to annihilate the bowler whose pace had now dwindled to generous. Three fours and a single to keep strike at the change of the over. He had less joy with young Tom Tarry, who bowled a good line and length to frustrate entirely the eager batsman. Only two runs for a misfield at fine leg and only eight overs remained with O'Connor to bowl to the uncelebrated Stevie Whiteman. Creek required 57 runs for victory off 48 balls. The game was poised delicately, the scales able to tilt in favour of either side.

'What on earth was that?' Parry Taylor thought to himself, thinking a passing wood-pigeon had dispatched a half volley on to the top of his head.

'Not rain, surely, there's hardly a cloud in the sky,' wondered Peter Jackson.

'Thank goodness,' thought the weary Joe Robbins, quite redundant in the outfield.

'Shit!' murmured Vince Clayton, feeling in a good

batting mood and seeing the cricket ball like a pumpkin.

The raindrops were silent at first, until they multiplied like falling rabbits and hit the outfield with a thump, one after the other. Merely a summer shower, suggested the home team, nothing much to worry about.

'It's pissing down,' exclaimed a Creek player, interpreting the same conditions.

Within a few minutes a dark cloud had appeared overhead and players were scampering from the field with hunched backs and screwed-up eyes. It poured down for the best part of a quarter of an hour. Birds flapped wet feathers and beaks as they searched for dry branches. The village church bell struck six-thirty, but surprisingly, nobody left the meadow for their other commitments. Tarry's spin bowling had speeded the over rate along considerably, and though they had spoken at tea of a few welcome hours in the Plough Hotel, the conversation in the pavilion had switched to the possibilities of further play. It was anybody's game, but a rained-off draw was hardly a good result for either side. There was little glory in such a dampened finale.

'Don't worry, it's only a shower,' promised Geoffrey Baird. 'These are only passing clouds,' he assured the throng. And there was every chance that he was right when one recalled all that he knew with regards the passing of anybody or anything through the Little Dow parish.

Molly Martin lifted her head from its cushion of dandelions and undergrowth and looked into the eyes of her new lover.

''Ere, Julian . . .' she quizzed.

'Yeah?'

'Can you feel what I feel?' she asked.

''Doubt it, darling, you ain't got what I've got, have ya?' he joked.

Molly broke into thunderous laughter, aggravating her

smoker's cough. She brought her knee up accidentally, but most unkindly, her hair bedraggled by running water and running fingers.

'You saucy devil!' she exclaimed. 'Can you feel the rain, I mean?'

'Yeah. So what?'

'Well, if it's raining they won't be playing no cricket,' she prophesised.

'And if they ain't playing none of the old Jiminy Rabbit, then your mum and dad will be wondering where on earth you've got to, won't they?' he deduced.

'Yeah, they will. Blimey, Julian I've had it.'

'Yeah, three times actually, darling,' the sporty wag corrected her.

They both laughed and rolled in each other's arms before turning turtle and rising to standard height. They adjusted their dress as though entering a party, then set off in search of anyone who may have wondered where they had got to, no longer caring whether or not their whirlwind romance remained a secret. They crossed the jewelled outfield in the easing rain, and arrived hand in hand at the pavilion steps. The rain had cooled Julian off somewhat, for which he was grateful.

Not a soul commented upon the lovers' arrival in the pavilion, and Molly's parents were nowhere to be seen. Rain had stopped play for most, but two in particular had barely noticed. They sipped a piping hot cup of tea, and winked at each other whenever their eyes met.

'I don't think I could take much more,' sighed Molly.

Elsewhere, there was polite banter until the rain eased once and for all and the umpires set off for a quick wicket inspection before play finally resumed. Aubrey Padgett followed, just in case a light roller was necessary. He pretended to hope not, for it was a messy job clutching the rust-ridden handle of the ancient implement. Of course, deep down he longed for any responsibility, but Lily Grace sent him back like a scolded dog, allocating him the final duty of shuffling the tin numbers before placing them in order on the wet grass.

Lily told most of Buckinghamshire that play was to resume in three minutes. The rain had moved off to dampen the evening spirits of the would-be-barbecue set of Oxford, leaving a wet wicket across which the ball would skid unpredictably. It was perfect for a fast bowler. Vince Clayton predicted the return of Trevor White, but Jackson unfortunately hadn't even considered this obvious option. Clayton and Whiteman were padding up again, quite surprised by the abrupt halt of rain. Winston Waites was resuming his low-key profile — it really hadn't been his day. He chatted quietly to the two batsmen as they crouched on one knee, securing the pads on their legs with the straps and buckles that still remained after five seasons.

'Come on, lads, we're nearly there now,' he enthused. 'Any half-raspberries that come your way, just smack 'em to the ropes. That little spinner's only a saucepan, don't let him get the better of you, Vince.'

'Leave it out, Winston. What do you take me for, my son?'

'Yeah, I know . . . I'm sorry, Vince mate, but all of a sudden this bleedin' game means a hell of a lot to me OK?' Winston confided.

'Sure man, leave it to me, I fancy a bit of a slog. Stevie, you ready, me old China?' he asked his partner.

'Nearly, guv,' promised Whiteman, who didn't really want to go in again if the ball was going to come at him faster because of the shower.

Vince crouched and continued, 'Stevie, try and snick a single and get me the strike. Get it?'

'Got it!' he replied with a feeling of great importance. Stevie Whiteman was not a man of many words. He used all the ones he knew with great regularity, but his vocabulary was comparatively sparse.

'Good luck, lads,' said Waites as he patted the two

batsmen of infinitely varying ability on the back as they marched into battle, leaving footmarks in their wake on the soggy outfield. 'Don't forget, 57 to win!'

Geoffrey Baird replaced Nicholas O'Connor, Jackson hoping the dampened wicket would turn the ball. Baird was a mediocre bowler who disguised his inability rather well with an impressive run-up to the wicket. Stevie Whiteman played to orders, pushing the first ball to nowhere in particular for the necessary single. Clayton clapped him with one gloved hand and a bat.

'That's the way,' yelled Winston from the ropes. Whiteman was delighted. He had moved up to 5 and looked, by his standards, in good form.

Clayton looked around, choosing the destination of the next ball. He thought about the river, then realised the loss of time would hardly be advantageous to Creek. Against Smythe's red wall, what a good idea.

Baird flighted one teasingly. It took hours to reach the anxious batsman. Clayton called on all the strength he had as he swung his bat like a golf club. The ball rose limply to second slip where even a player as useless as his lordship could hug it to his chest. Vince Clayton was out and neither he nor Lord Smutsy could hardly believe their luck. Clayton had no idea what had gone wrong with his intended smash beyond the ozone layer, but the ball had simply bounced on its seam and caused him to play the wrong line. Peter Jackson ran over to pat the catcher painfully on the back with his giant gloves as Vince Clayton set off for the pavilion, swaggering with embarrassment. Baird was looking more and more the man of the match with every minute.

'Unlucky, Vince,' consoled his side as the villagers warmly applauded his entertaining knock of 36.

'That bleedin' bowler, he's a right Jodrell Banker if you ask me. Gawd knows how he got me out. It *must* have been *my* fault. Sorry, Win, looks like I've gone and blown it for you. Shame, me old china, 'cause it's a beautiful raffle ticket, nice and slow and the ball bounces true . . . well, it *did* anyway . . . Out to that stupid berk, I can't believe it! Oi, Rudi, got any Bob?'

Creek's batting strengths sulked back at the pavilion, reflecting upon what might have been. Montgomery Holt, wicket-keeper supreme, batted like wicket-keepers do. Jim Parks, Godfrey Evans, Rodney Marsh. Anything could happen and occasionally it did. Monty was in much the same mould, lots of strength, a good eye, only he missed the ball more times than he hit it. With 56 still needed and Stevie Whiteman at the other end, Winston was excused to feel a little despondent after such fine morning and afternoon sessions. Monty's team-mates wished their keeper the best of luck as he strode in. He had even strapped on a pair of *white* pads, such was the seriousness of the occasion. But Winston forgot to wish him well; he was down and his side was nearly out. His nostrils twitched.

'Rudi! Go and smoke that somewhere else. I can smell it from here. Try and be a little bit discreet, man.'

'Sorry, Winston old chap. Wanna tug?' his saucy brother asked.

'Bollocks,' replied the Creek Cricket Club captain without discretion.

Of Baird's remaining four balls, Monty played and missed three, and though he hit the fourth he wasn't quite sure where, so he preferred not to run. Unfortunately it was an easy single which would have given him the strike at the other end.

Lord Smythe crouched even lower in the slips and more enthusiastically. 56 off 42 balls now, and the Little Dow players and supporters were quietly confident. The Creek side were well browned off.

It was now an all-slow spin attack with Baird at one end and Tarry at the other. Tom Tarry was too young to recall the halcyon days of Lock and Laker, but it hardly mattered because the similarities were confined to Tom's flannels, which were a little baggy around the crutch like Jim Laker's always were.

CREEK CRICKET CLUB SCORE WITH SEVEN OVERS REMAINING

Stevenson	*ct Jackson*	*b O'Connor*	*25*
Peters		*b White*	*8*
Clayton	*ct Smythe*	*b Baird*	*36*
Pinder		*b White*	*1*
Waites R.	*LBW*	*b Tarry*	*18*
Waites W.	*ct Jackson*	*b Tarry*	*0*
Whiteman	*not out*		*5*
Holt	*not out*		*0*
extras			*4*
TOTAL			*97 for 6 wickets*

The situation favoured Little Dow, only four wickets remaining (three and a half if the exhausted Julian Jannik was taken into account).

Tension, rather than lack of energy, lost Tarry his line and length at the crucial time. His control went, too aware that every spectator and player were staring at each delivery. He felt sick, and his errors were such that even Stevie Whiteman welcomed the deliveries with open arms and guard. The flattered number seven bat took ten off the over to register his highest score of the season, a smart 15. It was unusual for him to trouble the scorer, though to Aubrey Padgett nothing was any trouble. Tarry took his sweater and walked to the boundary, head held low. Peter Jackson was not too displeased to see the boy so miserable; it meant he cared about his performance and he wouldn't bowl so untidily again in a hurry. He had made a fine discovery in Tom Tarry, a youngster who would play for Little Dow for many years to come. Young Tom hadn't done his job prospects much harm either, for Lord Smythe was as proud as Jackson that one of his staff had excelled for the village at the game of gentlemen. Tarry had that one-up, one-down for life, or certainly until the head gardener pushed up the daisies, in which case the workers' cottage would be his. A good spell by the new boy, despite the final wayward over, and the players confirmed their appreciation with light applause as he searched for the arms of his sweater.

Peter Jackson knew that a single off each remaining ball was insufficient for Creek. He made the obvious move, sending his fielders out to the watery regions of the outfield. Nine fielders encircled the wicket some twenty yards or so in from the boundary. Baird bowled: Monty took a single, Whiteman took a single, Monty took a single, Whiteman another, Monty added one more and after a few minutes of sprinting hither and thither by the batsmen, it was Geoffrey Baird's last ball of the over. He had contained Monty and Whiteman rather well, and was more than content with his contribution. He lobbed the ball towards Stevie once more.

'Sod this for a game of soldiers,' muttered Whiteman, 'I'm putting this one into the river.'

He smacked a six and although it never reached the river, if Julian and Molly hadn't moved from their love-nest the broad-shouldered athlete would have got a turbo-charged cricket ball on his backside. However, it would probably have brought the tears to *Molly*'s eyes. It was 118 for 6, leaving a target of 35 runs off the remaining 30 deiveries.

The six-hit had brought cheers and somersaults from the higher members of the batting order back in the pavilion.

Lord Smythe, disgruntled at being moved from second slip, clutched and soothed his lumbar regions. It had been a long day in the field, and what with taking that magnificent catch at full length, its ferocity almost breaking his index finger, he was pretty wiped out. In all fairness his interest hadn't waned, and he crouched to gather in the snick of his next victim off the thin edge. He was very deep now, some thirty-five yards from the bat, but he crouched all the same — he thought he had to!

Stevie Whiteman patted tiny fragments of dirt on the strip; he was doing everything by the book. He had watched Baird take his sweater from the umpire and waddle off like a demented octopus struggling to connect the correct white arm with the correct white sleeve. A compact and thorough over with little flair or imagination, exactly what the astute Jackson had expected from his *bête noir*.

Trevor White was back in business (as was his wife, no doubt on some new location). He and his captain stood at the bowler's end discussing the field. He tugged at his beard, deep in concentration as he'd seen Mike Hendrick do. There they stood, hands on hips like two porcelain egg-cups in the distance. Men moved towards where the fingers pointed. With one hand Trevor gestured the new placements with the other he wiped the battered ball on the front of his white flannels. He preferred new balls as they gave more turn both in the air and off the seam, particularly when only the one side had been polished but Trevor should have bowled at the resumption of play, and Jackson now realised it. To allow Stevie Whiteman to get his eye in was a blunder on somebody's part. But Trevor hadn't bowled for the best part of two hours, so he was fresh and two yards faster.

He stormed in and was unlucky not to take Monty with his first delivery. The swashbuckling keeper played too late but the ball brushed off his bat down to third man and he picked up two runs as Joe Robbins sprinted round to retrieve it. He threw in with all his might so that the ball only bounced twice before plopping into Eddie's waiting gloves. Monty's luck didn't hold out. He skied Trevor's next short-pitched offering and the ball lifted away to . . . oh no . . . Lord Smythe. Jackson closed his eyes and waited for the roars or the groans. Lord Smutsy hadn't taken a catch all season until earlier that innings, and he had never taken two in the same game before in his whole life. Would he do it?

'Owzat!' shrieked the village. He had.

Lord Smythe couldn't believe it, he felt like throwing the ball into the air like his beloved Cowdrey would have done, but he had appearances to keep up. Instead he tossed the ball ten inches or so from one hand to the other, dropped it and groaned as he bent down to retrieve it. Lord Smythe always presented the man of the match with a bottle of fine port or claret, but this had made the presentation a little difficult, for without a shadow of doubt Smythe considered himself to be that very man.

Montgomery Holt's innings had been short and sweet, though a little longer in duration than the standard Bob Taylor knock, but he knew more had been asked of him by Winston Waites. It was more or less all over bar the bar of the Plough Hotel. Alfie Donald had never hit a boundary in his life and the two remaining batsmen had deficiencies too — Pumps Parker in brainpower and Julian Jannik in stamina. Julian didn't really feel like holding up an end, as he'd been doing that all day.

Curious spectators gathered around the scorer for an update of the situation. Aubrey enjoyed the attention, scribbling furiously in the book and sprinting across to change a tin number.

Alfie Donald didn't smile as he joined his chum Stevie Whiteman in the middle. There were reputations at stake, and beneath his façade Donald was a sensitive man who wished he was better at just about everything he did. He was determined to have a go. After all, it was only a case of giving strike to Stevie.

'How many runs do we need now?' asked Rudi Waites.

Aubrey Padgett silently showed him the scorebook, tapping his pencil where the current total was registered. It didn't look too promising. Rudi thought he had more chance of kissing Mrs Robbins than seeing Alfie Donald hit a boundary.

Stevenson	*ct Jackson*	*b O'Connor*	*25*
Peters		*b White*	*8*
Clayton	*ct Smythe*	*b Baird*	*36*
Pinder		*b White*	*1*
Waites R.	*LBW*	*b Tarry*	*18*
Waites W.	*ct Jackson*	*b Tarry*	*0*
Whiteman	*not out*		*23*
Holt	*ct Smythe*	*b White*	*5*
Donald	*not out*		*0*
extras			*4*
TOTAL			*120 for 7 wickets*

Creek needed 33 runs for victory, but now Trevor White had returned to bowl. It looked grimmer by the minute for Creek, as Whiteman had already batted well beyond the call of duty or his capability.

Trevor White ran in to Alfie Donald, the field a little closer owing to the arrival of the new batsman. Donald seemed to be finding it increasingly difficult to get the ball away for the planned single, well aware that Stevie Whiteman was backing up almost halfway down the wicket, and then sprinting back to avoid a run-out. By the end of the over the luckless Donald hadn't disturbed the scorer. Little Dow fieldsmen grinned smugly: 33 runs off 24 balls was a tall order for men of the lower order.

Geoffrey Baird strode in and presented his cap to Parry Taylor before the nod from Jackson to continue.

'It was sheer delight to be behind the stumps as Trevor hurtled in on his slightly curved run. He bowled very well; as accurate as I had ever seen, as consistent as human failings allowed. He had caused Monty Holt to play wildly and, quite honestly, I felt he was worth rather more than the two wickets he had claimed. I cupped the keeper's gloves at stomach height and felt the thud as one of his deliveries sunk into the leather. It was a tremendous feeling, made me wonder what it must have been like to keep wicket when Trueman or Statham were bowling. Despite the heavy gloves and the inner gloves, I bet the bloody ball didn't half sting when it slapped itself into the keeper's palm after one of that pair's efforts.

It must also be added that I felt quite confident we would win the match, probably before the allotted overs too. I took Tom Tarry off at the oak-tree end because we were entering the most crucial part of the game and I wasn't convinced that his nerve would hold. A few wayward deliveries could swing the game Creek's way, but I couldn't see how they would pull this one out of the fire, even allowing for the last over from Lord Smythe, which normally turned out to be a complete fiasco.'

Peter Jackson was absolutely right; Tom Tarry had bowled admirably, taking the wickets of the Waites brothers, two of the most dangerous batsmen in the Creek side. He had conceded a few runs in the process, but such significant wickets are rarely cheap. The sacrifice of 38 runs was more than acceptable.

Tarry had learned to bowl with an antique ball that his father had picked up at a garage sale. Its former owner had obviously played a bit in his lifetime and Tom reckoned there was every chance the ball had been awarded to him for particularly good bowling figures, maybe even a pre-war hat-trick. The youngster had used the ball to master the art of spin; of sending the ball both ways; of flighting and keeping a low trajectory. He aimed at an old green oil drum, hardly Oxbridge stuff but effective all the same.

The late Tarry senior hadn't known which sport used such a heavy ball. He thought perhaps one of those Irish games of which only Irishmen understood the rules; maybe the ball was styled for miniature bowls. Obviously

Tom's father had never been a sporty type; his pastimes seldom straying beyond taking a few trout from another's brook or trapping a rabbit in another's snare. Cricket was an unknown quantity to him, so he used the ball for breaking the ice on the water barrel outside his crippled, stumbling cottage. It proved to be far more hygienic than slinging a rusty mallet into the frozen layer. What was more, the ball always floated back to the top once it had served its purpose. A most wonderful invention, the cricket ball.

Geoffrey Baird came in to bowl to Stevie Whiteman. According to Winston Waites, nobody was too certain how Stevie retained his place in the side, yet he did. This was the first decent knock he had managed during two seasons with Winston and his friends. They all thought him a nice guy, and that was probably a factor helping his selection.

So it was the most pleasant Stevie Whiteman facing up to the most unpleasant Geoffrey Baird.

Whiteman continued where he had left off, calmly taking 6 runs off the first two balls of the over. He was batting like a demon, his measured shots flying in all directions, some towards the intended areas, others not. The crowd hadn't seen such an exciting climax to a game at Little Dow for many a day; most ended in draws, others were washed out, but this was something else altogether. To be half an hour from stumps, still not daring to guess who would win, was truly nail-biting stuff. Pipes puffed furiously and bottom lips were bitten as Trevor continued the over.

Molly Martin and Julian Jannik huddled together on the bottom pavilion step. There was a slight chill rising in the evening air and it was beginning to cut through the spectators, but neither they nor the players noticed. She ran her hand along Julian's inside-leg measurement, staring lovingly into his eyes.

'Julian, what's going to happen to us,' she asked.

'Nothing much, you'll probably lose by a dozen runs or so, unless that bowler . . .'

'No, Julian, not what's going to happen in the cricket, what's going to happen to Molly Martin and Julian Jannik?'

'Oh *us*, dunno really, me old darling. Why? What do *you* think's going to happen to us?' enquired Julian, steering the ball into her court.

'Don't know, Julian, what would you *like* to happen to us?' she continued. It was becoming tedious, like a Don Mosey commentary on a Glamorgan *v* Warwickshire three-day game.

'Dunno, Molly. West Ham's a bleedin' long way from Little Dow. I suppose we could meet up now and then, halfway or something like that, eh? Other times, if I could lay me hands on some wheels I could drive over here. That's a good idea, ain't it?'

'Of course it is, but listen *I've* got a car, what about my visiting you back in West Ham? It wouldn't take more than an hour and a half down the motorway. That seems to make far more sense to me,' enthused Molly.

'You've got a jam-jar, eh? Blimey, girl, all this time and I never even knew. That's fantastic.'

'Yes, Julian, all this time, all seven or eight hours. Now listen, do you want me to come and visit you or not? Just tell me if it's a one-night stand or a little more to you.'

'Listen, Molly, you don't want to come down the East End to see me now, do you? What would all the people what live round here say about that? Besides, they'd nick the wheels off your motor round my way, then you wouldn't be able to get back home again. No . . . I'll come out and see you again sometime. I give you my word, Molly,' Julian whispered, pecking the girl on the cheek.

'Julian, are you keeping something from me?' she asked. 'You're not married are you?'

'Don't be daft, Molly. Me married? You want your bleedin' brown bread examined. You have got to be joking, girl. I am definitely NOT married. All right?'

'Then why the reluctance about my visit?' Molly begged, stroking his tightly curled hair.

'Well, it's like this, darling. Where I live ain't too hot really, specially compared to a classy gaff like Little Dow. To be perfectly honest . . .' Before he could conclude the obvious, Miss Martin interrupted with a hint of anger in her voice.

'Don't come that one, Julian, I've met Londoners before, and specially East Enders. They're the proudest bunch of people I know. Besides, I wouldn't care if you lived in the proverbial shoebox in the middle of the road. It's not important to me. Come on, tell me the truth now, you are married, yes?'

'No. I am not married, I am not engaged, but I have got a lady back home. Having said that, she couldn't clean your bleedin' boots.'

'I'm not wearing boots,' Molly observed.

'All right then, darn your tights.'

'What's she doing while you are here playing cricket? I suppose you've left her at home to do the weekend shopping and clean your house or wherever you live,' suggested the inquisitive girl, who loaded the question with three or four bullets.

'Matter of fact, she ain't at home today,' chuckled Julian. 'She's gone away for the weekend. She's swimming up and down Loch Ness. That is if her broomstick got her that far.'

Julian tried to recall other chauvinistic gags he had heard at the Circus Tavern in Essex. It wasn't his usual style, but he enjoyed the deviation, to get back at the delicious nosey-parker.

'What's her name, Julian?' she persisted.

'No, it's not Julian,' he replied. 'I can't remember what it is now,' he giggled. 'Oh come on, darling, give it a rest, eh? She's back there and I'm here with you. I wasn't to know I would meet you, was I? But we *did* meet and that's all that's important right now.' He kissed his beautiful Miss Molly.

Her curiosity was still not satisfied. 'That's all very well, but what if she was to appear round the bend of the river right this very moment. That would be a bit awkward, wouldn't it? What would you say to her then?'

'Well, to be perfectly honest I think I'd ask her to pad up and bat instead of Pumps Parker,' Julian replied with a self-appreciative chuckle.

'You know what, you are hopeless, honestly.'

'Yeah, just like Pumps Parker,' he concluded.

Molly finally realised she was batting on a sticky wicket. She chose to drop the subject. And that was that, except that Julian had remembered another wicked story. It was odd how he became facetious at the tenderest moments, switching from sympathy to sexism in one foul gag.

'Do you know, Molly,' he said, 'when I got home from work the other day my girl friend asked me if I noticed anything different about her. I looked at her hair, clothes, etc. I wasn't sure. D'you know what I mean? I said to her, "You've had your hair done?"

"No."

"New dress?"

"I'm not wearing a dress."

"You've plucked your eyebrows?"

"No."

"You're not wearing a bra?"

"No, you don't know, do you?"

"No idea, come on then, what's different?"

"I'm wearing a gas mask!"'

Julian laughed loudly, causing the deep fielders to check the zip of their flannels. He was not usually so chauvinistic, but it seemed a good laugh at the time. He had totally lost track of the proceedings and he sidled away from Molly, still chuckling away to himself to visit Aubrey Padgett for an update.

Stevenson	*ct Jackson*	*b O'Connor*	*25*
Peters		*b White*	*8*
Clayton	*ct Smythe*	*b Baird*	*36*
Pinder		*b White*	*1*
Waites R.	*LBW*	*b Tarry*	*18*
Waites W.	*ct Jackson*	*b Tarry*	*0*
Whiteman	*not out*		*29*
Holt	*ct Smythe*	*b White*	*5*
Donald	*not out*		*0*
extras			*4*
TOTAL			*126 for 7 wickets*

Geoffrey Baird then produced what must have been the most significant over of the whole day. It was a uniquely splendid spell of bowling by him which foxed poor old Alfie Donald. He played and missed six times, and six times the bails remained intact. It was the turning point of the whole game; Creek were hardly in a position to allow Little Dow's bowlers the luxury of a maiden over. Baird was delighted with himself as he flung the ball back to Trevor White, who was still feeling the pinch from his previous over, what with Baird taking such a short time to complete his maiden.

Alfie Donald and Stevie Whiteman met between the two sets of stumps, their faces tense and concerned.

Twenty-seven runs were still required from the eighteen remaining balls. The Little Dow fielders were on their toes, three overs from a well-deserved victory. It was not a time for making mistakes. One more over each from Trevor White and Geoffrey Baird, then the final assault from Lord Smythe, as was the village tradition. Little Dow customs hardly matched up to the church gatherings at West Meon for Thomas Lord, nor the traditional Ashes compaigns, but in its own way Lord Smythe's final six-ball contribution was as respected as those. It seemed the partnership between Whiteman and Donald would prove abortive.

Aubrey Padgett remembered the splendid stand during the 1943–44 season when Worrell and Goddard put on a best-partnership performance of 502 unbeaten runs. Sir Frank made 308 not out, and Able Seaman Padgett sailed to more troubled waters with the splendid achievement etched deep enough into his memory to last the duration of the Second World War. It was hard to recall that a man such as Padgett had fought for King and Country. Curiously he was stationed at Hambledon at peacetime, drank at the 'Bat and Ball' public house and wallowed in the streets around the first village cricket green. What stories he could tell if the inclination allowed, but alas the miserable Padgett closed off his past, choosing only to please the noble Smythe in the present.

Trevor White and Peter Jackson deliberated at the pavilion end. Lily Grace moved in from the square-leg umpiring station, completely blocking the sun from the Little Dow captain's eyes, thus helping him as he scanned the outfield. He thought how strange it was that the meadow grew to vast proportions whenever he had gaps to fill in the field. As a batsman, he hadn't spotted such cavernous openings. Jackson felt as he had a quarter of an hour previously, that singles were of no use to the opposition. And of course he was right; the asking rate had increased to exactly one and a half runs per ball for the three remaining overs. A daunting task for the inexperienced East End fledglings.

'What do you think, Stevie?' asked a nervous Alfie Donald.

'Dunno really, but I could do with a Jimmy Riddle. What do you think?'

'No, not here,' replied the gullible Donald.

'Not the Jimmy, you silly sod, the situation. What do you think we should do?'

'Well, why don't you go for a boundary, and I'll try to get a few singles. Then whoever's left at the last over can have a bit of a crack off whoever's bowling.'

'I tell you,' beamed Whiteman, 'that ain't such a bad idea. Let's give it a go.'

'Geronimo!' yelled Donald, and the two returned to their respective creases, but there was no passing Red Indian to answer his call.

Peter Jackson stationed every fielder with the exception of Trevor and himself back on the boundary ropes.

'And don't forget, chaps, walk in as Trevor comes in; we can afford to give away a few singles but no twos,' shouted Jackson in a completely uncharacteristic way.

Trevor shuffled his feet, arched his wide shoulders and in he ran, gathering momentum with every stride. His hair trailed behind, as did his shirt tail, until, with all the warrior-like panache of Dennis Lillee, he released a torpedo of a delivery towards Stevie Whiteman. Whiteman prepared himself, feet well apart, skilfully balancing his short frame. The bat went forward, adjacent to the front pad. An admirable style . . . but Jackson had taken the ball before Stevie completed the stroke, and had lobbed it back to the bowler.

'Go on, my son, have a go,' pleaded Winston under his breath.

'Come on, Stevie, your moment of glory,' said Stevie to his inattentive self as the bowler trod the familiar path towards the stumps.

'This is it!' muttered the batsman, and this time he clouted the ball high over the bowler's head. Joe Baker gave chase but to no avail. The ball fell short of the ropes, and the cheeky Whiteman was furious that a much-needed six hadn't been scored. Lily Grace wriggled her hand in a snake movement, Aubrey Padgett took the pencil from his mouth, raised it in confirmation and four precious runs were added to the score.

He should really have been caught, that being the reason why Little Dow were positioned in the outfield, but Baker J. hadn't caught anything since he was in the army. Stevie loved the applause that echoed through the still of the evening. The anglers had gone home and a few ducks quacked irritably as they searched the bank for crusts or crumbs. Jackson could see that every cricketer was concentrating hard, that every cricketer was petrified, and this was only village-green level. Oh what torture it must be to play at Lord's with thousands of spectators, some drunk, some not, scanning everybody for a misfield or a bad return throw. Hell must be the only word, he thought.

It was becoming very chilly as Alfie Donald took a new guard of middle against Trevor White. The childish mannerisms had been eliminated by the tail-ender, for he had never been set such a challenge before in his life. He yearned for success and he yearned for a toilet, such was the strain.

'Good straight bat now,' advised Whiteman.

'This bat's already straight,' pleaded Donald. 'I ain't got to go and get another one, have I?' he asked his superior.

'Alfie, a good straight bat is a bit of cricket talk, a bit of the old Jiminy Rabbit. Don't swing, just guide the ball away. All right, my son?'

Twenty-three still to get. Trevor came in at the anticipated pace — less fast than usual. He was intent only on good line and length, those were his instructions. Containment was more important than wickets now. He passed the static frame of the umpire with pounding footsteps until he reached the crease, where he groaned and leapt skyward before releasing another rip-roaring delivery from a perfect sidways on stance. The ball left his hand and he groaned louder, like a highly professional wrestler, then watched the good ball skid off the cropped grass and home in on the waiting batsman. Donald played the sort of stroke never before witnessed by any attending player or spectator. The ball walloped him hard on an unprotected thigh muscle, an inch or so above his front pad.

'Balls!' screamed the wounded Donald.

'No, but damned close!' rejoined Baird.

'Run, Alfie, for Christ's sake run,' screamed Stevie as he sprinted down the strip with the tired bowler. The ball sat motionless a foot or so from the stumps. Peter Jackson and Trevor White both tried in vain to reach the ball before Whiteman had made his ground, but it was too late, Stevie had made it. The Creek players cheered the action.

'They're throwing the game away now,' overstated one attentive villager.

'Always do,' piped in another know-all wag.

Alfie Donald was off the mark, with a shiner of a purple bruise guaranteed the next day. 22 they chased, but Trevor bowled far too well for the second-raters. No more runs off the over. Only twelve balls remained. Winston's enthusiasm was draining from somewhere close to his armpits.

'Any special strategy?' asked Geoffrey Baird, tossing the worn-out ball from one palm to the other.

'Just keep it tight, Geoffrey, and we're there. Don't worry about a wicket, just keep the runs down, that's all that's important.'

'Bugger that for a game of ruddy soldiers,' thought Baird, realising easy wickets were there for the taking. He wanted the man of the match award, and after his stylish knock he felt sure that a few wickets for good measure would secure the prize. The game was all over, bar the shouting and drinking. 'Go on, old boy,' he muttered to himself as he walked back to his bowling mark, 'he's all yours.'

Baird rubbed the ball, and Donald rubbed close to his. He had the same fault with his batting as Tony Greig, lifting the bat high as the bowler came in. Any good yorker was unplayable with such a style, and that was the kind of delivery, Baird realised, that would send Donald packing (as opposed to sending Tony Greig packering).

The field stayed as it was with the exception of Philip Trevelyan and Barnaby Baker, two of Little Dow's finest fielders, who moved across to the off side. Parry Taylor juggled with his six stones for the last time as he stared down at the bowler's crease. Baird had a final check of his field. He waited confidently, with his body weight on one leg and his buttocks protruding. He wiped his forehead and smothered the sweat on to the ball. He wasn't sure what it did, but as Jeff Thomson and Sarfraz did it regularly there had to be a good reason. Baird stood just over six feet, a size he attributed to many hours spent pruning tomatoes in his greenhouse. Suddenly Parry Taylor lowered his arm and Baird, as if cleared through customs, was set to pass.

A couple of hundred eyes were on Baird at that moment and he loved every rich second. Beyond the boundary a few walking sticks shook unsteadily as weary legs rested on wooden chairs adjacent to the pavilion. The vacant deckchairs were far more comfortable but a little frightening to the older villagers. The sound of creaking bones and exhausted strength was a regular backdrop to the meadow as the old folk tried to raise themselves from the multi-coloured traps. This had been rather a special day for them, for with the exception of Trevor White's wife, it was unlikely that any member of the Little Dow community had ever witnessed such a captivating day's sport.

The Reverend Jonathan Tyler bounded across the meadow like a spring lamb, his continuous smile displaying his large, twinkling teeth. He knew as many cricket rules as Winston Waites knew Commandments.

'Aha, Aubrey, my good fellow, how goes it?' he asked politely.

'The end is nigh!' replied Padgett, far too innocent to appreciate his own wit.

'Jolly good show. I always said so, didn't I?' chuckled the man of the cloth to the man behind the pencil.

'Jolly good,' the vicar muttered a second time as he turned to see Geoffrey Baird trotting into the stumps with renewed vigour.

Mrs White had also arrived to study progress, wondering what time her Trevor would like his customary Saturday roast. She failed to grab his attention as he concentrated on the job in hand, as *she* had been doing most of the day. She turned and disappeared through the jumbled undergrowth between meadow and river, intent on placing the Yorkshire pudding in the oven, regardless of the state of play. She was ravenous, which wasn't surprising given the energy she had burned up that afternoon. Mrs White also needed to make up her weary face, which Rudi Waites had noticed earlier and described as 'worthy'. Let it never be said what the good lady thought of the possibility of an afternoon session with the big black lad. Suffice to say that if they made a film of her thoughts, there was little doubt the leading role would go to Joan Collins.

Baird's first ball of the over was too long. Alfie Donald hit it with all the strength his frame could muster and took a single as the ball rolled down to deep extra cover. It was returned by Joe Baker who usually threw wide and under arm. Donald had doubled his score and for the next delivery Baird doubled his pace. Whiteman mistimed his stroke and his attempted hook off the short ball would have fallen into the gullet of a second slip; it could have given Lord Smythe a hat trick! Peter Jackson gave chase, biting his giant glove away from his hand in the process. Another single and Donald, though backing up admirably, was feeling a little worn out.

'I'll get you this time,' whispered Baird, reaching his white metal marker and turning to race in towards the unsuspecting Donald.

A wayward delivery it was, a less than medium-paced full-toss, and the grateful tail-ender smacked the ball back over the bowler's head, scattering the deckchair brigade and the star-spangled vicar. It was six runs, confirmed by Parry Taylor's raised arms. The Creek boys yelled and jigged in response to the unexpected long hop.

'Go on, my son, let's have another one like that,' begged Winston.

'Hit the bastard into the river,' suggested Rudi, with considerably less aplomb.

Jackson was not pleased with Baird's performance, for he was not playing to orders, but he said nothing. Only 14 needed from the final 9 balls. It still looked hopeful for Little Dow, but victory for Creek was a real possibility.

Alfie Donald turned to Lily Grace, ''Ere, darling, was that a six I just got?'

'Yes, young man, and a good shot it was too,' she replied.

'Blimey, all the games of Jiminy I've played and I've never scored a bleedin' six in me life,' Donald confessed to the buxom official.

'Well, you have now,' Lily confirmed.

'Yeah, not half, and I'm gonna get another one in a minute,' he boasted.

But on the last ball of the over Donald offered a dolly to Trevelyan and he was caught without the addition of any further runs. He was applauded as warmly as a war hero returning from the battlefield. He had batted far beyond the call of duty. He had even taken guard and worn a box.

'Good knock,' acclaimed Winston as team-mates gathered to pat Alfie Donald's back.

'What a shot, eh? Six all the way that,' beamed Pumps Parker, who had never struck a four, let alone a half dozen.

'How many did I get, guv?' yelled the ecstatic Donald to Aubrey Padgett.

'Eight, I'm afraid,' came the reply.

'Could have batted longer, Win, but I was busting for a piss,' revealed the hero as he knelt before the vicar to remove his pads.

'Good shot, my man,' the Reverend proclaimed.

'Cheers, Vic,' said Alfie Donald smiling.

'Over and out!' yelled Parry Taylor.

Nobody noticed his pun; Little Dow were busy congratulating Geoffrey Baird, and Creek were engrossed in back slapping their Alfie. Parry shrugged his shoulders and limped off towards the square-leg position. The one-legged umpire hoped he would have the opportunity to use the phrase again, but the odds were stacked well against him.

Julian Jannik was next man in. He was pretty useful with a bat, far better than many that went in higher up the order, but he welcomed the long rest after a particularly aggressive bowling stint. He didn't make a habit of pulling spectators on the boundary, but having done so, the prolonged rest was even more welcome.

Julian was in no rush to get to the wicket. Besides he could only find one batting glove. Vince Clayton scampered around searching for a pair as Julian casually strapped the second pad to his second leg.

'Julian, will you forget me after tonight?' Molly asked.

'Leave it out, Molly, what a time to ask me that, just when I'm going in.'

'I'm sorry, love, but I have to know,' Molly sulked.

He comforted her with a giant arm around her shoulders, then they quickly nestled together before the new batsman rose to begin the long walk to the middle.

'Tell you what, Molly, I've been thinking,' he turned and continued. 'It's like this you see. I'm in and out of jobs in the East End. I ain't got no serious bird, like, and I was thinking . . . um . . . what if I was to try and get a job round here? I could get me own pad, perhaps be a gamekeeper's assistant or something where they throw in digs. Then we'd see lots of each other, wouldn't we?'

Before Molly could answer he was on his way, stepping smartly towards the wicket, glancing at the sky for more light and inspiration. She simply could not believe her ears. She pinched the top of her leg and it hurt; yes, it was really happening to her. She knew her lover was embarrassed; it had taken the best part of forty overs to come out with that little gem. It was just as well he had been called into duty.

Julian took guard and patted the crease, determined to have a crack at the required total. Silence fell across the meadow, a few ducks flew overhead, cringing as they waited for the sound of shotgun and the sting of pellet. They were surprised it never came, because it usually did. They loved cricket, too.

There was no cricket talk around the ropes, for anxiety had silenced the on-lookers. It was the last over.

Stevenson	*ct Jackson*	*b O'Connor*	*25*
Peters		*b White*	*8*
Clayton	*ct Smythe*	*b Baird*	*36*
Pinder		*b White*	*1*
Waites R.	*LBW*	*b Tarry*	*18*
Waites W.	*ct Jackson*	*b Tarry*	*0*
Whiteman	*not out*		*34 (career best)*
Holt	*ct Smythe*	*b White*	*5*
Donald	*ct Trevelyan*	*b Baird*	*8 (career best)*
Jannik	*not out*		*0*
extras			*4*
TOTAL			*139 for 8 wickets*

There had been admirable bowling by Tom Tarry, Trevor White and Geoffrey Baird, each man taking at least two wickets. Nicholas O'Connor, although only having taken one, had done his side a good favour by dismissing the volatile Slogger Stevenson as he was getting his eye in.

Peter Jackson pondered, rubbing his chin with his wicket-keeper's glove.

> 'To be perfectly honest I didn't know what to do. Lord Smythe always bowled the final over, but never before had the final six balls been so crucial. Trevor White was the man for the job, keeping good line and length, containing the eager batsmen. Lord Smythe? Definitely not. He had never taken a wicket in his chequered career, yet the last over went to him without question.

Perhaps he would be content with the two splendid catches he had taken in the field, perhaps this time around he too would appreciate the gravity of the situation and pass. Trevor White approached hesitantly, well knowing the predicament I was in. He had played for the village many many times before and knew the rules of his lordship. He was more than keen and willing to get the final few minutes over and done with.

Lord Smythe waddled over. Would he hand over his rightful ritual or would he bloody well hold us to it?'

— FIVE —

The Final Over

As is often the case with the new-style one-day cricket, the final over proved to be the most dramatic sequence of batting and bowling of the day's play.

Julian Jannik joined Stevie Whiteman, who was stoned out of his mind on his 34 not out, halfway between the two sets of stumps.

'What's the situation, Julian?' asked Whiteman.

'We need 14 runs off these last six balls to win. Can't really see it myself, but we might as well have a go, eh?' Julian replied.

'You bet.'

The pair strolled back to their respective action stations, patting and prodding at the cropped strip as they went. Normally a blue joke or similar was swapped in the middle during overs, but no such humour filled the darkening evening air. The light was fading, though few players noticed. It was obvious, however, to batsmen and spectators, who had to screw up their eyes to focus on the participants in their illuminating whites, which shone as though struck with the glow of fairytale moonbeams.

In the warmth of the Plough Hotel the landlord rubbed spotless glasses, checked full shelves of cigars and cigarettes, wondering what had happened to the white-flannelled invasion. The sardine sandwiches were beginning to curl at the edges as the weary dough struggled to escape from the unhealthy aroma of the trapped shoals. Hot toddy and French onion soup would probably have been more warmly appreciated by the chilled cricketers, having seen off one shoal of fish at tea.

'Look, Julian, why don't I tap a single and give you strike?' suggested the nervous Stevie.

'Leave it out, my son, all them runs you've got there, you get on with it. Finish 'em off once and for all, that's what I say,' Julian retorted.

'All right then,' said Whiteman with a wry grin.

Trevor White dared to walk across to the advancing Lord Smythe to offer his continued services at the pavilion end.

'I think, to be honest, Lord Smythe, I think it's my last over, isn't it?'

'I think to be equally honest and blunt, young man, I think it's my meadow we are playing on,' the offended landowner warned. 'I shall take the final over as usual, Peter,' he roared authoritatively.

'Very well, Lord Smutsy,' conceded the wicket-keeper. 'Very well.'

Peter Jackson moved from his position behind the stumps to the aid of his bowling change. He shuffled his cricket boots with embarrassment, more than surprised that the timid, well-mannered Trevor White had breached the accepted tradition that it was Lord Smythe's bowl. Trevor was absolutely right, of course, the fat so-and-so should not be allowed to bowl the last six balls. Little Dow had worked hard — all that time in the outfield, all that fine batting — and now it was to be thrown away at the very end in the guise of Lord Smythe, bowler. It was a debacle an absolute joke, yet nobody laughed. Some of the Creek side giggled and sniggered when they understood the problem, but they had never seen how truly pathetic a bowler the rich man was. The replaced bowler thought Jackson needed his head examined, and so did Jackson. But he knew which side of his cricket bat was buttered, for without Lord Smythe's generous free rental of the meadow, there would be no Little Dow Cricket Club. He couldn't overlook such kindness.

Heads fell sadly amongst the on-lookers as they realised what was happening.

'Any prayers left?' Mrs Robbins asked Reverend Jonathan Tyler.

'Only a small one, nothing as mighty as that which is required here, I'm afraid,' he replied, appreciating the caustic sarcasm of the old lady.

Smythe always kept the same field as the previous over. It seemed to make sense, because it saved time and hid the fact that the bowler didn't know any of the titles given to field placements. Fine adjustments were impossible given such ignorance of the more subtle points of the game.

Back on the boundary Trevor White picked his nose furiously and wished the ball were a hand grenade as he flicked it in the general direction of his replacement bowler.

What did he bowl? Good point. Lord Smythe professed to be a man of spin, right arm over the wicket, leg-breaks. Sadly his bowling style was no longer as relevant to the game, especially the one-day match, as it had been in the days of the Empire. The fact that left a massive question mark by the side of Lord Smythe's description of himself as a spin bowler was that the ball never turned, not an inch did it turn. He simply bowled very slow, very short and not very straight. He had never taken a wicket so his average was difficult to ascertain; nor had he ever *nearly* taken a wicket, so it was equally difficult to measure the amount of bad luck involved. His deliveries could be crashed to the boundary with great ease by any player worth his salt with the bat. In Smythe's favour, the two that represented Creek Cricket Club at that moment were somewhat below the salt, which at least made for a fair contest, but it brought teeth marks of utter frustration to the bottom lips of observing villagers, be they players or not. Boundary fielders felt they were too close to the batsmen and chose to retreat ten feet or so, and Lord Smythe registered his disgust at their lack of confidence. But they were adamant. If village cricketers had a union they would certainly have been out.

Lord Smythe rubbed the ball on his portly gut (he had owned his flannels far too long to subject them to that awful red dye). Lily Grace's arm was held out once more as Stevie Whiteman surveyed the field. There were very few gaps, and hardly surprising too considering every player excepting the bowler and keeper was on the boundary. There were singles for the taking but they wouldn't be enough for victory. More players patrolled to the off than the leg side. Whiteman with rare perceptiveness took a new guard of off stump. Lily Grace shrugged and moaned at the request, never having placed a bat so far to the left before. He completely hid the stumps from the bowler.

'I say, Lily old girl,' asked Lord Smythe, 'is there any law that suggests he should move back a little?'

'I'm afraid not, Reggie . . . um . . . your lordship, but it's fair to say that if the ball touches the pads it will be leg-before-wicket without question. That much I can assure you.'

'Think I'll go for that one then,' hinted Lord Smythe, as he took a handkerchief from his pocket to wipe his leaking brow. He hadn't even bowled a ball yet, but he looked worn out. Decidedly unfit, he was a health hazard not only to himself but to the multitudes who had gathered around the boundary ropes to witness the final scene.

Jackson crouched ten yards behind the stumps, prepared to sprint for any snick towards the slips area. He was nimble enough to do so, but he knew his pre-emptiveness would be of no use. Any bowler who couldn't smack one of Lord Smythe's deliveries to the ropes deserved to be hanged.

Lord Smythe to Stevie Whiteman.

'Right arm over the wicket, six to come,' orated Lily Grace, delighted to officiate such a significant over.

Lord Smythe didn't take a run-up, more lolloped like a hippopotamus towards the stumps; no chance of a foot fault here. Lily Grace was at his end and they were the fondest of friends. Rumours had even suggested some sort of an affair, a generation or so ago. In came Lord Smythe, slowly, deliberately, searching for the first ever wicket of his long but not distinguished cricket career. The ball left his hand like a marshmallow and fell towards the ground — hopelessly wide. Stevie Whiteman tried to lift it for four or six, but couldn't reach far enough across to make contact. Rudi Waites and Vince Clayton groaned on the boundary — they would have wrapped the ball round the Oxford one-way system. Lily Grace thought long and hard, then against her better judgement she held out her arms, signalling a wide delivery to Aubrey Padgett, whose pencil had been raised long before.

'A little wide, I'm afraid,' she mentioned to Smythe.

'Quite right, Lily old girl, quite right, damn well slipped. Only just wide though, eh? Only just?'

'Only just,' agreed Lily Grace, a woman who was as astute at cricket as she was at choosing her cosmetics.

'Unlucky your lordship, good length,' yelled Jackson.

'Yes good length, Smutsy,' seconded Geoffrey Baird.

'You wanker,' muttered Trevor, watching his hard work disappear up in smoke.

'I'm coming round the wicket this time,' warned Lord Smythe to anyone who cared to listen. Six deliveries to come, and only twelve to win. Whiteman didn't need to change his guard — he wouldn't have known what to change it to anyway — though middle and leg would have been a more sensible guard against a more sensible bowler. Lily Grace looked at the crease as Lord Smythe's ancient boot appeared, then her eyes rose to follow the flight path of the next ball.

'Oh no. It's damn slippery here,' insisted Smythe as his second delivery went five feet the other way, well beyond leg stump.

Two wides from two balls, and things were looking bleak for the villagers. Still six balls to follow and the score diminishing with every pathetic delivery. Creek players tittered, Little Dowers held their heads in despair, afraid to follow the wayward missile. Smutsy had tried both over and round the wicket. All that remained was for him to call for a chair and bowl on top of the wicket, then all options would have been explored. But he returned to over the stumps and his third ball was good in comparison; it crawled towards the batsman at a rate of half a knot. Even if it had hit the wicket it is doubtful that it would have dislodged a bail. It seemed at least a minute before Whiteman swung at the leather snail, but he mistimed his annihilation and the ball limped through the trimmed square for a single on the on side, wide of Tarry.

Eleven runs were needed off the last five balls of Lord Smythe's session. Local supporters slumped in deckchairs, pondering upon what might have been. A resounding victory had all but been reversed. Stevie Whiteman, never one to fling the bat around for more than a few minutes, cursed the fact he had managed only a single. One run was a tremendous bonus to his season's average, but the untalented batsman knew it should really have been a four or even a six, all things considered. On the other hand, Julian Jannik, who had already seen more action than he had ever expected, was delighted to be tapping the popping crease at the receiving end. He glanced across to the scoreboard, then to

Molly who waved discreetly from the boundary steps, then he crouched to face the next sloppy delivery.

Lord Smythe rubbed the ball on his flannels and licked his index finger as he wrapped a flabby right hand around the uncontrollable cricket ball. The whole meadow waited in trepidation. Where was this one going to go? Lord Smythe was in no hurry, relishing the moment. If only he could win the match for Little Dow. He knew his cricketing credibility hardly matched his social standing — suffice to say it barely came up to Tom Tarry's social standing — but one wicket would change all that. He bounded to the crease, his foot a good six inches over the line. Lily Grace ignored the unlawful step and watched the ball as it left the bowler's hand in the general direction of the stumps. Lord Smythe farted, almost managing to follow through with his follow through. Lily ignored that too.

Everybody was transfixed by the lame projectile for what seemed an eternity as it bounced wearily on the wicket. Julian threw his front leg forward and swung loftily at the ball. There was a massive crack as leather collided with willow. The ball shot into the air — sixty feet, seventy feet, it seemed like two hundred feet — before it decided to return from its orbit to nestle in the long grass to the right of the pavilion. Six runs all the way. The Creek boys yelled and hooted like crazed limbo dancers at a beach party as Lily Grace raised her arms, revealing her suspender belt for the last time that day.

'Shot!' screamed Winston Waites, delighted at the way the game had turned in his side's favour.

'Go on, my son!' urged Rudi as Julian returned to his crease, prodding nonchalantly at tiny divots on the wicket.

'You're beautiful,' whispered Molly Martin to her far-distant lover. Lord Smythe could not share her jubilation.

'Blast!' he complained. 'If he hadn't have got that tickle the damn ball would have uprooted the off stump. Well played, young man,' he called to Julian, much to the utter bewilderment of the outfield.

It was a stupid ball which deserved every one of the six runs it gave away. It should have been twelve runs in fairness but Creek were in no mood for complaining. Julian was off the mark, and how. Lord Smythe gathered the ball at the second attempt, allowing Trevelyan's throw to bounce three times to remove the sting. Five runs to win off four balls. Jackson looked deeply concerned as he left his wicket-keeping position to confer with his bowler.

> 'It had been an unfortunate decision by Lord Smutsy to take the last over. My position as Little Dow captain meant nothing compared with the rights of the meadow owner, but I thought the great man may well have waived the last rites on this particular occasion. Victory had been there for the taking, now it had disappeared beneath the shambling bowling of one fat nobleman. Our only chance of avoiding defeat was for Lord Smythe to suffer a timely heart-attack or damage a knee ligament. Many would have actually preferred the former at that moment, though I would have settled gratefully for the latter. From my vantage point behind the stumps I can confirm I hadn't seen such ridiculous bowling since Graham Gooch's impersonations in that final Test Match over at the Oval. Lord Smythe strolled towards me as a silenced meadow hoped and prayed for rain or an accident. I thought it only right to meet the man at the middle of the wicket, though in truth I would have preferred to have walked in the opposite direction and thrown myself in the River Thames.'

Lord Smythe and his captain, Peter Jackson, met mid-over, mid-stumps. The conversation was obvious. Little Dow, once so convincingly poised for a smooth victory, were on the brink. More or less a single each ball would swing it for Creek Cricket Club. What were the fielding side to do about it? That was the cause for concern, the reason why the two players had gathered in the middle in what was for Little Dow a most untraditional way. Four balls remained as both batsmen rendezvoused for a tactical chin-wag. Smythe's eyes scanned the outfield while Julian and Stevie chuckled, their nerves eased by his lordship's pathetic attempts at turning his arm.

'You all right, Stevie?' asked Julian.

'Yep, never had double figures before. What about you?'

'Not so bad, a bit cream crackered though. It's been a long old day,' replied a man who was keen to get back on the extra-curricular job, just as quickly as his size-twelve cricket boots could carry him.

They glanced at the other two who stood a few yards away, deep in conversation. It must have been only six or seven feet that separated the two pairs yet they were as distant as two planets, almost as far apart as Boycott and Illingworth.

'What do you reckon they're talking about, Julian?' asked the inquisitive batsman with the excellent new batting average.

'Dunno, probably thinking about bowling underarm. Don't really care, just so long as they bleedin' well get on with it. I want another quick Donald before we slope off home.'

'Good was she, Julian?'

'Piss off and mind your own business,' suggested Julian coolly. The batsmen parted company amicably and headed towards their respective stumps. Winston and the London boys on the boundary ropes were most impressed with the players' decision to discuss the few remaining balls, even though victory was imminent. The bowler and his captain were still conferring.

'What do you think, Peter old boy?' Smythe asked.

'Not sure, I must admit. Looks like we're on a bit of a sticky wicket. I think we are forced to bring in the field to save the singles. If we do that you *must* concentrate on line and length,' insisted the kind Jackson who was restraining himself from insulting the landowner and returning to his keeper's position.

'Yes, Peter old boy, think you're absolutely right there. Line and length, that's obviously the answer. Should have used them before, I suppose, instead of attacking the weaknesses of the batsmen. Should have got a wicket really, but even that would not have secured the darned game, would it?' he asked.

Jackson did not have the foggiest idea what fat Smutsy was talking about but he nodded all the same.

'Good line and length,' reminded Jackson as he set off back to his position.

'Thanks, Peter old boy, but I think you're being a fraction kind there. Not one of my better performances really, eh?' asked Smythe.

Jackson reached the popping crease, where his eyes met Julian Jannik's.

'How's it going, man?' enquired the friendly Julian.

'Oh, truly wonderful, truly wonderful. That chap bowling to you is so thick-skinned he'd only sneeze if you shoved a bloody hand grenade up his nostrils.'

'Know what you mean there, my friend,' endorsed the black batsman. 'Say no more.'

Smythe had waddled to the start of his run-up. Lily Grace held out her arm like a piece of an iron.

'Just to remind you all, it is right arm over the wicket, four balls to come,' she yelled towards Berkshire and Oxfordshire.

'Yes, unfortunately we are only too aware of that,' retorted the bitter Trevor White.

Lily Grace and Lord Smythe turned their heads in unison to identify the foolhardy person who had uttered such truisms. The guilty party stood motionless as two pairs of eyes burned through his outer skin like a dose of radium. He didn't care, for he was well past caring; all he wanted now was dinner and a few hours in his workshop, taking out his frustrations on his Chicago harmonium with hammer and chisel. His wife had been curing her cravings and frustrations throughout that summer's day, and Trevor deserved similar in the evening.

Trevor White was well and truly cheesed off, and indeed the nine other innocent parties in the field weren't exactly savouring Lord Smythe's antics. He now trotted in and bowled his fourth ball and the over's second delivery. It only bounced once before reaching the bat of the delighted Julian Jannik. Smythe's bowling was becoming a little tighter, but it was still a dolly for the athletic Julian. He smashed the ball through the covers for the second boundary of his three-minute innings. Not a solitary villager applauded the most delightful stroke of the day's play, because it was no longer pleasurable to clap the men who were annihilating the dreadful bowling so ruthlessly. The Creek contingent yelled and screamed as before; the game was almost sewn up. Julian moved to double figures as Trevor White, now a Rebel With a Cause, set off at a leisurely pace to retrieve the bruised ball. He showed quite clearly his complete disgust at the whole fiasco by walking there and walking slowly back, probably a distance of eighty yards or more, then placing the ball very deliberately in the hand of the unimpressed bowler.

However, Lord Smythe was thoroughly enjoying every single moment of his over. It was now at a crucial stage, the kind of challenge he relished. Only the one run needed off three balls. There was no time for cowards out there. Smythe had helped in the securing of the Empire (and some say the screwing of the umpire) and this was the ultimate challenge. He had crouched at the bowler's end after each delivery, his backside as wide as a sight-screen, just in case the possibility of a run-out arose. Whether or not he understood that boundaries cancelled out such possibilities was questionable.

One run for glory. Time for drastic changes in the field.

Barnaby Baker was ordered forward to silly point — incredibly silly with such a bowler — and began to panic.

'What about that gap on the boundary?' he pleaded to Peter Jackson.

'It's probably only for one ball,' hinted Jackson. 'Please do as he asks or he'll blame us for the dreadful over.'

'All right then, Peter, but if that ruddy ball fractures my skull it's you they are going to want to talk to, you know. Eleven more deliveries and you could become a mass murderer,' said Barnaby Baker grimly.

He thought of home, just as he had during the Second World War. His evening meal would be served in half an hour, so he had no intentions of being whisked away to the local casualty department with his head held underneath his arm. It was all right in the Bloody Tower, but not on the Bloody Cricket Pitch.

Parry Taylor's stones had gone haywire (a reference to his counting aids, not his kidneys). He no longer had any idea how many balls remained but chose to keep silent at his position wide of square leg. After all, Lily no doubt had her own small heap of gravel.

'How many, Parry?' she asked.

'Damn,' muttered Taylor. 'Better check with the scorer, my dear,' he suggested.

'How many balls to go?' she yelled with a vast bellow from the lungs. Aubrey glanced down at the sorry sight of a recorded Little Dow defeat to check.

'Three, maybe more, who can say?' he answered in an uncharacteristically imprecise way. His sullen voice was far removed from his grovelling character. It was all of a sudden far easier to associate him with the aggressive tattoos which decorated his arms.

Lord Smythe rubbed the well-hammered ball once again for no apparent reason. Jim Laker himself often stated the stupidity of a spin bowler to keep any sort of shine on a cricket ball, and after all a spin bowler was what Lord

Smythe pretended to be. Laker knew only too well about the benefits of a dull ball. Here it was more a case of a dull bowler.

Reginald Smythe to Julian Jannik.

'No ball!' shrieked Lily Grace as his lordship wildly overstepped the mark.

'No WHAT?' bellowed the annoyed man.

'No ball,' repeated the umpire at great risk to her person.

'Don't be so stupid woman, that was a fine delivery if you ask me,' insisted Lord Smythe.

While the debate continued Julian Jannik had swung at the ball but mis-hit it, and it trickled off a thinnish edge through to Peter Jackson behind the stumps. Lord Smythe had scored the final run for Creek Cricket Club. The outfield stood as still as a photograph, momentarily having no idea that the game had been thrown away by an illegal delivery.

Creek Cricket Club had won the match.

Lily Grace removed the bails, thanking the players for their time, the meadow came to life once more and the Little Dow fielders set off, heads low, towards the pavilion. By rights, it was to be their day of glory, but Lord Smythe had turned the tide and the odds. Jackson removed his brightly-coloured keeper's gloves, wiped his brow with relief that the whole business had come to an end and made his way to the game's post-mortem.

Lord Smythe, utterly dejected, grabbed his sleeved and sleeveless sweaters from the plentiful waist of Lily Grace, his face burning with anger.

'That was a stupid decision, Lily old girl, what on earth possessed you to yell such a thing?' he asked.

'Well, you may not realise it, Reggie, but in actual fact I did you a darn good favour. Well . . . I meant to anyway,' she replied in her defence.

'What on earth do you mean?' he roared.

'Let's face it, Reggie, that black chap was a good batsman so by no-balling you I gave Creek the one run they needed and would most certainly have got with one of your last three balls, and in the process I helped to maintain your bowling average.'

Lord Smythe paused, impressed by the irrefutable logic.

'Good Lord, hadn't thought of that. Thanks awfully, Lily, I owe you a gin and tonic for that,' the grateful bowler confessed.

'Quite so, anytime you like,' offered Grace.

'Well, how about some time when Lady Smythe is off on one of her shopping expeditions in St Tropez?' suggested Lord Smythe, confirming the rumours that were whispered through the lanes and culs-de-sac of Little Dow.

'That *would* be nice, Reggie,' whispered the beaming lady, 'that would be really nice.'

She touched his arm gently as they both giggled at the thought of what would follow.

> 'As I left the field I was certain I had captained Little Dow for the very last time. Usually I simply humoured the pathetic man, but that over had been the final straw for this camel's back. It had made a mockery of a game that simply did not deserve such a ridiculous finale. It was like bringing on unicyclists and impressionists at the end of Hamlet. It was not the right time to say my piece, not wanting to ruin the Creek side's victory, but come the next cricket club meeting at the Plough, I would hand in my resignation to anybody who had taken the trouble to attend.'

The Creek players cheered each other and danced around like Sydney hillbillies. Pumps Parker, in particular, loved every minute and hugged all he could lay his hands upon. Lord Smythe headed towards the Range

Rover, bright red with fatigue and embarrassment. He was off to find the medals he had purchased for all the players in the contest.

Aubrey Padgett hastily calculated his way through the final knocks and bowling averages, and had completed the task by the time the triumphant batsmen peered over his shoulders, curious to learn of their own tallies. Aubrey turned the neat page back to the Creek innings and there it was, plain for all to see.

CREEK CRICKET CLUB

Stevenson	*ct Jackson*	*b O'Connor*	*25*
Peters		*b White*	*8*
Clayton	*ct Smythe*	*b Baird*	*36*
Pinder		*b White*	*1*
Waites R.	*LBW*	*b Tarry*	*18*
Waites W.	*ct Jackson*	*b Tarry*	*0*
Whiteman	*not out*		*38*
Holt	*ct Smythe*	*b White*	*5*
Donald	*ct Trevelyan*	*b Baird*	*8*
Jannik	*not out*		*10*
extras			*5*
TOTAL			*154 for 8 wickets*

CREEK CRICKET CLUB WON BY TWO WICKETS

154 when they only needed 153? Nobody seemed to be sure what had happened about the extra run, but there seemed little point in worrying about it now, with the exception of Aubrey Padgett who had never made a scoring error in his life. Twice he re-checked the book, twice it came to the same score. But it was all quite irrelevant, Julian Jannik would certainly have hit another six before the game was over. Padgett closed the book quickly and scurried off to hide in the visitors' changing room. It was empty. The Creek players were dancing

around the outfield which looked like a scene from Carnival.

The match was over; Creek Cricket Club had stolen it, against the odds, on Lord Smythe's final erratic over. Now the heated discussions would commence and the Plough Hotel would resound with the banterings of both the victorious and defeated, the bar awash with accusations and 'if onlys'. But that was all later, the light was failing badly and the presentation of medals and man of the match award needed to be made. The players changed hastily, Creek men hardly noticing the whimpering Padgett in the corner. Winston Waites, victorious captain, shook each of his players warmly by the hand. Lord Smythe set off in the general direction of the manor to collect the prizes being donated by his own good self.

Aubrey Padgett was the saddest man in the world. He left the excited throng and paced home, studying the footpath of the river. The shouts and yells grew fainter as he turned the bend and set off down the road towards his mother's house. While celebrations continued that evening, Aubrey Padgett wept himself into a migraine and lay in his bed, his head pounding with the cruel regularity of a bass drum at Creek Cricket Club disco. Some say the whole affair was the downfall of Aubrey Padgett. He was only ever seen after the match when he collected for National Lifeboat Day. He felt his credibility was gone, even though none of the other villagers were aware of the lost run anyway. Such was the obsessiveness of his pedantry.

Creek had won by two wickets and Peter Jackson was the first to congratulate his office junior.

'Well played, Winston lad,' he said, warmly offering his hand to the jubilant boy.

'Cheers, Mr Jackson, but I'll tell you what, it would have been a bleedin' sight easier if you'd owned up about that supposed catch that got me out,' he replied.

'What catch was that, Winston?' asked Peter Jackson playfully. 'Let's have some respect for our elders, shall we?' he suggested.

'Bollocks!' cried Winston Waites . . . then they both broke into hearty laughter and patted each other's back.

— SIX —

Post-Match Pomp and Ceremony

The powerful purr of the V8 engine could be heard in the distance as the generous Lord Smythe returned to the field. Curious eyes turned to the two massive pillars which supported the wrought-iron gates to the estate where two white lions with hearts of stone stood guard. They had sat there for many years, nicknamed Tom and Jerry by the younger members of the village. They were completely unperturbed by the grand comings and goings. Lord Smythe would have loved a drawbridge at the site, but it would hardly have been in keeping with the tranquil setting. The Range Rover bounced and bumped its way over from the mid-wicket boundary. Smythe kept his headlights on full beam, a brilliant symbol of authority.

The ecstatic Winston Waites discussed umpiring standards with the defeated home captain, referring back with regularity to his own harsh dismissal. Jackson hardly responded, still quite embarrassed by the false appeal that had dismissed the office junior. It hardly mattered now that Creek were victorious, but it was a matter of principle to young Winston. He felt he had been cheated and was not prepared to let the matter drop.

One-legged Parry Taylor limped amongst the cricketers pleading leniency regarding any such comments. The standard of his umpiring was beyond dispute; it was his female counterpart who was the cause of the disgruntlement. Lily Grace had wisely hurried home without taking off either her white coat or her face, knowing she would be the subject of much post-match gossip among the players. Besides, her pussy needed attention and there was a rather good play on Radio 4.

> 'It was sad the way she was criticised. For she was in truth a charming woman who merely tended to stretch the limits of officialdom and authority too far. Her boldness and enthusiasm, the way she stood out in the middle, officiating in the greatest game of gentlemen — these were admirable. Forget your Rachel Hey-ho, Hey-ho, it's off to work we go. Cricket was a game for the landed gentry that had infiltrated into public schools throughout the land, then passed down to Commonwealth countries which were originally given no choice but to gather sides to play their owners. Full marks for Lily Grace's courage, even if some of the decisions she had made barely deserved half that score, and even if she hardly lived up to her cricketing surname. She'd probably done the right thing by disappearing early.
>
> As far as the final ball of the day is concerned, I wasn't certain what was going on out there at the time so am loath to comment on the incident. Parry Taylor had claimed he was unsighted too, a wise move by such an upstanding fellow with such excellent vision.'

The Range Rover swung left and screamed across the outfield in second gear. A couple of cygnets and their worried parents, who had been well-behaved during the match and were nosing around in the hope of a few crusts (such a welcome change to angler's maggots), became startled by the high-pitched whining of the giant engine and took off in utter disgust. Their wings pounded against the evening air as they passed overhead, low enough to cause a draft down the back of any person over six feet tall. Julian Jannik gazed at their beauty, explaining the sadness that surrounds the death of such a beautiful specimen. Molly Martin, a country girl born and bred, was only too familiar with such stories, but she nodded politely as Julian explained all.

Lord Reginald Smythe dismounted from his white mechanical stallion, looking a completely different fellow from the man who had lobbed half a dozen hopeless deliveries at the opposition. This was Lord Smythe the wealthy landowner, not Smutsy the second slip and rubbish bowler. A dapper country gentleman in expensive brogues, tweed hacking jacket and trout hat with attached relevant flies, Lord Smythe played his part well, his props ideal for the play in which he acted. At first he had been annoyed by his own bowling performance — even by his standards it had been a poor affair — but the anger had drained from his face to reveal red rosy cheeks and an equally rosy nose that betrayed his liking for a good vintage port. He walked around to the hatch-back of the vehicle, ignoring the admiring glances from both sides, and produced a large cardboard box that bore the label 'Lord Smythe — Little Dow'. That was all that was necessary for the package to reach the manor, even though it was a dreadful cycle up the drive for the poor old postman. Smutsy pulled the box a few yards and, exhausted but happy, placed it on the table vacated by Aubrey Padgett, the all but impeccable scorer. Out came the medals one by one, glistening in the fading light of the summer's evening. It was by no means dark, but the mist was rising on the Thames, and a few leafy bonfires threw a layer across the evening sky. The visiting team were staggered when they spotted the elegant blue presentation boxes. Then, like oysters, the boxes were opened to reveal the winners' medallions that would forever recall the splendid day's sport. Suddenly, everybody forgave the thoughtful Lord Smythe. His bowling was negligible but his generosity gave pause for thought. It was accepted as a wonderful gesture on his part.

The medals were displayed on the table in two lines, like ragged formation dancers in a television contest. The cricketers huddled together as close to the presentation table as they could. Lord Smythe picked up one memento to show to the excited Rudi Waites, who had never received a souvenir in his life but for a mild dose of the crabs at West Ham baths a few years earlier. Rudi read out the inscription to his team-mates, as if deciphering it was beyond their capacity.

Member of winning side.
Little Dow C.C. v Creek C.C.
Played at Smythe's Meadow

Followed by the date and the day, the glorious 16th June. Certainly nice keepsakes for all involved. True, his lordship had managed to plant his name on them, but what did it matter, it was his money that had bought them.

Despite the snide tales that abounded, Lord Smythe was a charming man. He liked to rule the roost, but this particular roost was his to rule. Every village of England seems to be the same; there simply *has* to be a Lord Smythe, otherwise the village hall would decay and the church would have no candles or daffodils at Sunday Service. His final over had meant much to him, one of the few moments of challenge in a life that was tediously comfortable and hastily passing him by. For a dozen or so afternoons every summer he was plain old Smutsy Smythe with the huge gut, just one of the lads . . . and that was much more important to him than yet another dinner party. He could forget the years which wasted away beneath the façade of a Botham-sized bank account, he could forget too his inability to play the game well. His only chance of getting a bowl was to make the stipulation he had, because he knew in his heart that no captain in his right mind would allow him to bowl. At the cost of losing the pitch and its upkeep, Little Dow Cricket Club had no choice, but Jackson was grateful for Smythe's sponsorship, and he in turn was delighted that the captain shrugged off his self-indulgence as a fact of village life. To compensate the team for selecting such a bad cricketer, Lord Smythe rewarded them well.

Over one hundred spectators remained to witness the presentation of the medals, the speeches and the £10 man of the match award. There was also the added bonus of the glistening trophy for which teams competed for each year — the Reginald Smythe Trophy! It stood resplendent, towering over its metallic counterparts like a headmaster at school assembly. Alfie Donald felt like running off with the tableware, his East End ways getting the better of him in this all-too-tempting situation. It was too much to handle for him and Creek Cricket Club looked like walking away with *all* the trophies.

The crowd moved in closer as Lord Smythe produced a scribbled speech from the inside pocket of his hacking jacket. The meadow fell silent and even the dubious members of the East End fraternity were on their very best behaviour.

Smythe complained of a frog in his throat and Rudi reminded him irreverently that a frog in the throat was better than a toad in the hole. A few sniggers then silence for the important man of Little Dow.

> 'Ladies and gentlemen, may I, firstly, thank you for turning out in such splendid numbers for today's game against Creek Cricket Club from London. Applause makes every bowler try that bit harder and makes every batsman hit that bit harder. This has been the intention of the Smythe Trophy and I hope in years to come the two sides will compete for this beautiful trophy with the determination and keenness shown on the cricket pitch

today. It has been a splendid afternoon for all of us. Naturally there have been a few disagreements, as a matter of fact I would like to speak to Lily Grace about that very subject, but I bet a pound to a penny, she's bugger . . . um . . . she has retired for the evening.'

The crowd giggled at the aside; a good move by Smythe, always the clever man with words, he had immediately broken the ice and removed the starchiness from the ceremony. The on-lookers visibly relaxed as he continued on his verbal way.

'Yes, thank you indeed for a good game. I would now ask the winning side to come forward and collect their medals, with their captain . . . er . . . Winston Waites last on to collect the trophy and hopefully grace our ears with a few tips on how to play the game. Ladies and gentlemen, please put your hands together for Creek Cricket Club.'

The spectators cheered heartily as the embarrassed bunch of little-hopers marched up for their awards. They went in batting order with Slogger at the front, Pumps Parker moving up to number seven and Winston, as requested, bringing up the rear, a gesture usually left to the promoted Pumps. Flashbulbs lit up the affair and Smythe smiled broadly throughout. Each player mimed a grateful thank you to his lordship and his villagers and left, leaving Winston Waites alone in the spotlight to collect the Smythe Trophy. He lifted it high and stood before the microphone.

'Ladies and gentlemen of Little Dow, me and me mates here would like to thank you all a bunch for being so kind, what with all the food and stuff. Also thanks for a great game of the old Jiminy, which is what we East Enders affectionately call this game. It's a game we take as seriously as we can. All right, I know that some of you thought we were messing about at times, but we don't often get the chance to have a good time like this, what with having to work overtime and all that kind of thing, but if we'd have lost we'd have been as sick as bleedin' parrots. Thanks for the hospitality, we'd love to come back next year and defend our title. Or however I say it, we accept the challenge. I'd also like me and me mates and you lot here to thank the ladies who did the spread. It was magic, honest. Any questions about how to play Jiminy will be answered over at the pub in ten minutes' time. Thanks again.'

The crowd warmly greeted Winston's kind words, even if in the gloom they needed sub-titles to understand most of them. His natural friendliness spilled through his speech, and the triumphant captain handed the microphone back to Lord Smythe, coughed nervously and left the spotlight. Mrs Robbins and Alice thanked him for the mention and Winston kissed them both. His brother Rudi called him a babysnatcher. Lord Smythe continued.

'Ladies and gentlemen, we now come to the familiar faces of our parish, in this case the faces of true and fair defeat. But wherever there are winners and so on . . . May I ask for a nice round of applause for your husbands, uncles and cousins . . . Little Dow Cricket Club.'

Up they trooped, off went the flashbulbs as before, a team pose for the pavilion wall and everybody was having a very good time. The medallions were identical but for the inscription which read . . .

Losers
Little Dow C.C. v Creek C.C.
Played at Smythe's Meadow
Saturday 16 June 19——

as an eternal reminder. Lord Smythe sneaked a medal into the ticket pocket of his own hacking jacket but nobody seemed to notice. He called upon Aubrey Padgett and Parry Taylor (he would have called Lily Grace had she been there) and presented each of them with a handsome cigarette lighter for their trouble. The two tea-ladies didn't go away empty-handed either, each receiving a presentation of lavender and talc. The meadow was dark but for a few torch bearers until Lord Smythe returned to his Range Rover and shone the main beam from boundary to boundary. He disappeared up his drive to his waiting guests, who were no doubt hungry, thirsty and furious by this time, while the others walked slowly downriver towards the Plough Hotel.

Memories were made of such a day, which everybody knew would be spoken of for many years to come. In the meantime, though, people were wondering about the man of the match award, and what had happened to it. It had surely been won by Geoffrey Baird who Lord Smythe disliked as much as Peter Jackson did. Baird was claimed to be a threat to his lordship's power in the area, though that was hard to believe. Before Baird's dismissal at the hands of the Waites brothers, caught by one and bowled by the other, he had knocked up a dashing 64 runs. His innings had set the game alight and was particularly impressive when the fine bowling by Creek was taken into consideration. What with that and the two wickets he had taken as Creek chased the winning runs, he was undoubtedly man of the match. And well he knew it too, edging closer and closer to the presentation area with smug expectancy.

'Little creep,' whispered Winston to Pumps Parker, who had contributed little to the game, neither bowling nor batting throughout the day.

'Yeah, look at the little shit. I reckon I should be man of the match,' boasted Pumps.

'Well, I thought it would be either you or that tart of an umpire,' said Pumps's captain.

The award, however, went to nobody as Lord Smythe disappeared through the gigantic gates that closed on his solitude and his dinner party, which was getting under way two hours late.

'Come on, my son, let's get down the old rub-a-dub-dub and sink a few Veras, shall we?' suggested Winston as he put his arm around the shoulders of the hopeless cause that was Pumps Parker.

'Come on, Pumps, I'll get you a ginger beer and make you feel at home,' he mused.

'Bollocks!' came the expected reply. 'What d'you mean, buying me a bleedin' ginger beer? Are you getting at me?' the disgruntled man asked.

'No, I ain't, Pumps, what would you *really* like then?'

'How about a jar of vaseline?'

'Leave it out, old son. I've had enough sport for one day,' urged Winston nervously. They both collapsed with laughter and Pumps Parker pinched Winston's backside. Winston pretended to like it but was in fact extremely scared.

Geoffrey Baird went home to re-enact the day's play to young David who, despite being twelfth man, was so disgusted by his non-selection he hadn't bothered to go to the meadow at all. Nobody noticed but Peter Jackson, and he didn't give a fig.

The Plough Hotel filled with players, spectators, gaping teenage girls and cricket hold-alls smelling of damp towels and sweaty white socks. The pints began to flow as the post-mortems increased in volume. Real ale was a rarity for the London boys, as was drinking in an hotel, albeit one a third of the size of the cement monstrosity where they drank in Ilford. Very few pints touched the sides of their mouths as the thirsty sportsmen clung to the bar.

The meadow was still; birds slept in motionless branches, and only a few stray rabbits and mice ventured across the outfield to look at the bowlers' run-ups and study the labrador's heap. Strains of Haydn wafted from Lord Smythe's dining-room to the huge red wall, but the delightful notes did not penetrate the brickwork. The Thames splashed gently against the reeds, disturbed only by the hunting rat scampering between deep extra cover and the line of sturdy oaks.

Aubrey Padgett, in bed with a migraine and the scorebook, relived every run in the hope of finding the mathematical error his pencil had made. Not until each run (and boundary) was accounted for could he write the match report for the village magazine and sleep contented. His mother wished her 43-year-old son would marry and produce a grandchild for her but his father knew that pigs couldn't fly. They watched the television with the sound on low, hoping it would not disturb poor Aubrey and bring him racing down the stairs with his scorebook and his anecdotes about the day's cricket.

Julian Jannik and Molly Martin sat alone in the saloon bar, not troubling the bartender as they had no spare hands to dig out money for liquid refreshment. Neither had intended to fall in love; for Julian it had been a quick "Donald" many miles from harm's way, for Molly it was her first sexual experience with a black man. She had loved every minute of it and only wished that Julian lived in the village. She thought they would never meet again and had accepted that the Creek mob were a bunch of rogues who had neither the time nor the inclination to be constant.

'I love you, Julian,' she whispered, realising her time with him was short and feeling rather sad.

'I think I'm feeling a bit the same,' came the unexpected reply.

Their embrace grew stronger, hands strayed once more, and suddenly Julian could have done with the next size up in Levis.

'Fancy coming outside for a stroll?' he asked.

'If I must,' she laughed, and they left quietly, unobserved by the rampant throng in the public bar who were making the most of the remaining couple of hours.

There would be an unofficial bar extension which was no problem for the landlord, as policemen rarely patrolled the sleepy hamlet, and those who did were grateful for a late-night stomach liner.

Julian and Molly strolled back to the meadow. It was strange how silent it all was. They lay together at mid-on and Julian glanced around for the prying eyes of Parry Taylor or Lily Grace. He made a joke about Parry getting his leg over which Molly didn't really understand, and from there on it was bliss all the way. The cropped square was hard on Julian's elbows but he shunned the discomfort as he settled down for his final session as night watchman.

'What does your mum think of black men?' he asked inquisitively.

'Don't rightly know. Don't think she's ever been out with one. Mind you, she's got no idea what she's missing.'

With the sardine sandwiches finally consumed back at the Plough, the Little Dow players prepared for the walk home to their respective cottages and the Creek players clamoured for the young female villagers who wanted to be walked home via the mid-wicket boundary. It had been agreed that the Creek entourage would leave for London at 3 am allowing the successful men to have a final fling and the drivers to sober up for the long drive home. Beds were offered by friendly locals, but the Londoners arrived as one and left as one, such was the tradition of the East Enders.

Trevor White hadn't gone for a drink, as he was far too hungry. He had finished his roast dinner and was ready to climb upstairs with his wife but she wasn't in the mood; she never was these days. He couldn't understand why. Mrs White covered her love-bites in the bathroom with baby powder, climbed into bed and fell fast asleep.

It was a perfect end to a perfect day, with all agreeing on a fixture on the same day the following year and hopefully for many years hence. Not a single member of the Creek side could remember the long drive home, not even the three drivers, but they all arrived in one piece. By Sunday afternoon, Little Dow was once again a collection of small, musty cottages with stick roofing and exposed beams. The main road was silent and stray dogs relieved themselves where magnificent catches had been taken the day before.

On Monday, Peter Jackson and Barnaby Baker relived the game from the sleepy countryside into Marylebone Station. Baker hadn't had a particularly good game but had enjoyed it all the same. Jackson spoke highly of Tom Tarry and numerous members of the Creek Club. Baker nodded reluctantly in agreement.

Peter Jackson, solicitor, commanded respect from his staff as he entered the brown and cream office of Little & Jackson (Solicitors). He looked fit and healthy as he strode past the desks of office staff.

'It's all right for him,' said a typist to Winston Waites. 'He lives in the bloody country and spends all weekends blasting heads off pheasants and quail, you know.'

'Does he really?' asked the attentive junior.

'Of course he does, I bet that's what he's been doing all this weekend while I've been stuck indoors baby-sitting for my sister.'

'Good morning, Judy, morning Winston,' hailed the boss.

'Morning, Mr Jackson,' replied Winston Waites.

'Good weekend, Judy?' enquired Peter Jackson.

'Really nice thank you, Mr Jackson,' pretended the girl.

'What about you, Winston? Did you get home from my place safely on Saturday night after all that booze you put away?'

'Oh yes thanks, Mr Jackson.'

Judy looked at Mr Jackson the solicitor, and then at Winston Waites the office junior, double-checked her glances and then typed away at one hundred words a minute, her face burning with embarrassment. What a shame Tipp Ex can't erase spoken words as easily as typed ones. Winston chuckled as Peter Jackson closed his office door, then continued with his mundane filing.

'I thought Winston might be embarrassed when I asked him about his journey home, but if his loud laughter was anything to go by, he certainly made the most of his first ever chance of one-upmanship.

On the whole, it had been a very successful occasion. The villagers spoke of the game for weeks, particularly Geoffrey Baird who asked all but Lord Smythe what had happened to the man of the match award. The Plough Hotel hadn't had such custom since Ossie Trentham's wake. Aubrey Padgett came clean about the extra run that had appeared in the scorebook and after plentiful leg-pulling, the Cricket Club committee decided to waive the whole shocking incident without so much as a front-page headline in the local paper. Poor old Aubrey, he just couldn't take a joke. His scorebooks were the neatest in the land, as accurate as was necessary, and detailed to the point of disbelief: bowling averages, batting averages, catches, throws over the stumps, duration of thunderstorms. I was surprised he didn't count and record the lumps of Stumper's shit in the outfield. One wayward run throughout the season and the poor bloke was suicidal. He offered to pay a fine for his misdeed, but I took a pint of best bitter off him eventually and the wretched little affair was forgotten once and for all.

There was a sequel the following year. Sunshine warmed the meadow as Little Dow and Creek competed once more for the Reginald Smythe Trophy, but it never had the friendly, pioneering spirit of that first fixture. Many of the original players were missing from both sides, so whenever the Creek challenge game was discussed on cold winter nights in the Plough Hotel it was always the first game that nostalgically sprung to our minds.

We all remembered that splendid knock by the late Joe Robbins, no doubt the greatest moment in his cricketing career. An unexpected heart-attack sent him scuttling to the village church outfield with more ceremony than he ever would have wanted. Mrs Robbins never recovered from the dreadful blow. At an emergency meeting of the cricket committee we decided to donate the gravestone, and though we tried hard to think of a fitting epitaph, few suggestions were in good taste. Trevor White, though a sensitive wood craftsman, was the biggest culprit of all, reeling off reams of tributes he had thought up one uninspiring afternoon.

This is where Joe Robbins is dumped.
By the Lord Almighty startlingly stumped.

Poor old Joe
What a way to go
He surely deserved
Just one for the throw

God raised his finger . . .
Joe Robbins was out.

The tasteless poetry went on and on until members of the committee had, quite frankly, heard enough. Joe was a simple man of simple means. Hyperbole and levity were not his forte, and he would never have understood such memorials. We plumped for a few words of kindness suggested by his good chum Joe Baker:

Joe Robbins
Village celebrity and cricketer
Sadly missed at the crease
Remembered with affection

Mrs Robbins dusted down the etched words regularly, and flowers surrounded the kind man's place of rest. His widow and Alice continued to provide refreshments for many years. Often I noticed her glance towards the outfield with moist eyes, wondering why her darling Joe had been taken from her. We wondered the same thing.

We managed to win the return match by four wickets, owing to a magnificent performance by Geoffrey Baird, now a local councillor. Once again, though, there was no man of the match award.

Slogger Stevenson returned with cricket flannels and scored another impressive forty or so. Vince Clayton had joined a Youth Opportunity Scheme and was working down in Wiltshire. His aggression and fine fielding were sadly missed by the Creek side. Screwball Pinder was there and hadn't improved. His hair was a little longer and his guard a little more wayward, but it was good to see him again. Montgomery Holt, the keeper with the claret and blue pads, got married between fixtures and arrived a dapper man with a very pregnant wife. He played well but married life had diluted his sense of occasion, replacing his somersaulting antics with sombre Alan Knott stretchings and swingings. Stevie Whiteman had developed into a really rather stunning batsman, promoted to number two to share the opening stand with Slogger Stevenson. Eddie Peters had broken both his legs in an unfortunate car crash and was laid up for most of the Spring, awaiting a court appearance for driving without a valid insurance policy and giving a false name to the police (he realised he had damaged his legs so he gave the name of Parry Taylor).

Rudi Waites was the same as ever, though his hair had been painstakingly ringletted in true Shirley Temple fashion. He was still out of work, and with the recession biting deeper and deeper into the factories and yards of the East End of London, I was later to follow up the possibility of his working for Lord Smythe on the estate. He was a popular chap amongst the villagers, and I relished the thought of him becoming a member of Little Dow Cricket Club. I would dream of us reaching Lord's for the finals of the Village Cup Competition, then thought of Joe Baker, Lord Smythe and a few others, and gave up the idea.

Winston Waites had been a credit to himself at Little & Jackson. His day-release course had done him no harm at all; he glided through mathematics and business studies with considerable ease and soon had a desk of his own from which he flung unwanted files at the new office junior. He was going steady with a girl whose name I never learned, for he affectionately referred to her as 'the old boiler' — apparently a term of endearment in the East End. He popped out to Little Dow a couple of times during the winter months, no doubt tired of the decaying streets of East London. He fancied living in the country, or so he told me.

Julian Jannik and Molly Martin brought home to us the most touching reminder of what that first game had been about; they had moved into a cosy cottage together at the back of Lamb Lane. There was hardly room to swing a cat, but that was no problem as neither wanted pets anyway. It was strange how nobody in the village raised an eyebrow at the thought of the two of them living together out of wedlock. Most of the villagers remembered Julian from the game and were touched by his good manners and keenness to help the youngsters with their cricketing techniques (shame he didn't show us old 'uns a thing or two, also!). He worked for a car hire company near Aylesbury, with the intention of setting up on his own as soon as he could find a backer. He chose to play for Little Dow for the return game, and although he took some stick from his old chums he was instrumental in turning the game our way.

Pumps Parker brought up the rear for the second successive year, together with Alfie Donald. In the first match Creek had won the game exploiting Alfie's batting prowess, but in the second match he was out to a magnificent Julian Jannik yorker, first ball. Pumps Parker gave himself another ten years to reach double figures after which he decided, he would retire, very hurt. His was one of the wickets Julian took that season. On seven different occasions he took five or more wickets, and scored five hundred and twenty-six runs, a damn good tally for our standard of cricket.

Little Dow's side made far more familiar reading than the Creek line-up. Only the mortgage repayments had changed *that* much over the past twelve months. The coming of Julian and the going of Joe Robbins were the sole significant changes to the village side. Baird bought another acre of pasture to raise pheasants, and his head increased in proportion. Other than that, much was the same but with several beer guts obvious where before they had been discreet.

I enjoy any game of cricket, the unhurried pace of the game, like the unchanging ritual of the guard at Buckingham Palace or the nightly round at the pub. It's all a comforting reassurance that while the world around us changes for the better but usually the worse, the essentials of the grand English life still remain. When the last ball of summer returns to the waiting gloves of the wicket-keeper, and nothing is left but the calculation of the season's averages, I glance through the Little Dow scorebook. I always pause to relive that day on Saturday, June 16th when Creek Cricket Club, an unknown bunch of black and white chaps from London's East End, turned up in three battered vehicles to take on the might of middle-aged, middle-class Little Dow. Bonded friendships were sealed that summer's day. Some batted as they never had before, putting as much fear into the fielding side as Denis Compton, a celebrated Arsenal footballer. Others bowled supremely beyond their ability. And then there was Lord Smythe — there will always be Lord Smythe — and let us hope there will always be the annual fixture when Creek Cricket Club race through the lanes of Buckinghamshire to challenge us for the Reginald Smythe Trophy.

I wonder what the lads are doing now. I may never see some of them again, but at least one winter's night every year I relive that day with them. The fixture will live on as will this story. Like Coleridge and Schubert I believe that anything of lasting value is of necessity unfinished.

Coleridge and Schubert? The Creek lads knew only of Brahms and Liszt.

Over and out . . .

LITTLE DOW Ist XI v CREEK CRICKET CLUB
FOR THE REGINALD SMYTHE TROPHY

LITTLE DOW

BAKER B.	CT DONALD	B JANNIK	16
1.1.1.2.4.1.1.1.2.1.1.			
BAKER J.		B WAITES R.	1
1.			
BAIRD G.	CT WAITES W.	B WAITES R.	64
4.1.1.4.2.3.1.1.1.4.4.1.4.2.1.1.1. 2.1.1.4.1.1.4.(50)1.4.1.1.3.4.			
JACKSON P.R.	CT PINDER	B WAITES W.	7
1.6.			
COPELAND J.	CT HOLT	B WAITES R.	2
1.1.			
TREVELYAN P.	CT DONALD	B JANNIK	12
1.1.1.1.2.1.1.1.2.1.			
TARRY T.	LBW	B JANNIK	0
WHITE T.A.		B JANNIK	1
1.			
O'CONNOR N.	CT HOLT	B JANNIK	16
1.6.4.1.2.1.1.			
LORD SMYTHE		B WAITES R.	2
2.			
ROBBINS J.	NOT OUT		20
4.4.4.4.4.			
EXTRAS			11
1.1.2.1.1.1.1.2.1.			
TOTAL			152 ALL OUT

CREEK CRICKET CLUB BOWLING FIGURES AND AVERAGES, PLUS FIELDING ACHIEVEMENTS, EXCLUDING THE MANY DROPPED CATCHES, BUT INCLUDING A MOST DUBIOUS LEG BEFORE WICKET DECISION

JANNIK J.	20 OVERS	2 MAIDENS	38 RUNS	5 WICKETS
WAITES R.	14 OVERS	1 MAIDEN	43 RUNS	4 WICKETS
WAITES W.	7 OVERS	0 MAIDENS	44 RUNS	1 WICKET
DONALD A.	1 OVER	0 MAIDENS	16 RUNS	0 WICKET

FIELD CATCHES

HOLT M.	2
DONALD A.	2
WAITES W.	1
PINDER S.	1
TOTAL NUMBER OF CATCHES	6

AT LUNCH, CREEK CRICKET CLUB STOOD AT 85 FOR 4 WICKETS. SANDWICHES AND SPREAD SUPPLIED BY MRS ROBBINS AND HER FRIEND ALICE WERE EXCELLENT, PARTICULARLY THE COTTAGE CHEESE AND CUCUMBER VARIETY.

CREEK CRICKET CLUB IN REPLY TO LITTLE DOW'S INNINGS

STEVENSON S.	CT JACKSON	B O'CONNOR	25
6.4.1.2.6.1.1.4.			
PETERS E.		B WHITE	8
2.3.1.1.1.			
CLAYTON V.	CT SMYTHE	B BAIRD	36
1.2.3.4.6.2.2.4.4.4.1.3.			
PINDER S.		B WHITE	1
1.			
WAITES R.	LBW	B TARRY	18
4.2.4.4.1.2.1.			
WAITES W.	CT JACKSON	B TARRY	0
WHITEMAN S.	NOT OUT		38
4.1.4.4.2.1.1.6.4.2.4.4.1.			
HOLT M.	CT SMYTHE	B WHITE	5
1.1.1.2.			
DONALD A.	CT TREVELYAN	B BAIRD	8
1.1.6.			
JANNIK J.	NOT OUT		10
6.4.			
EXTRAS			5
1.1.1.1.1.			
TOTAL			154 FOR 8

BOWLING FIGURES OF LITTLE DOW AFTER A FINE SPELL OF BOWLING WITHOUT GETTING THE BREAKS

WHITE T.	20 OVERS	4 MAIDENS	47 RUNS	3 WICKETS
BAIRD G.	9 OVERS	1 MAIDEN	30 RUNS	2 WICKETS
TARRY T.	9 OVERS	1 MAIDEN	28 RUNS	2 WICKETS
O'CONNOR N.	11 OVERS	0 MAIDEN	24 RUNS	1 WICKET
LORD SMYTHE	1 OVER	0 MAIDEN		

LOTS OF RUNS AND NO WICKET

CATCHES (NONE DROPPED THROUGHOUT THE INNINGS)

LORD SMYTHE	2
JACKSON P.	2
TREVELYAN P.	2

SPECIAL NOTE FOR THE FEWEST EXTRAS GIVEN AWAY AT A HOME FIXTURE IN THE LONG HISTORY OF LITTLE DOW CRICKET CLUB 5

GLOSSARY

Abandon hope	*soap*
Berk=Berkshire Hunt	*female pudenda*
Bit of a Glasgow=Glasgow ranger	*stranger*
Bit of an Oxford=Oxford brogue	*idle vagrant*
Bit of snatch	*an observed female spectator*
Boat=boat race	*countenance*
Bright and frisky	*whisky*
Bristols=Bristol Citys	*mammary glands*
Brahms & Liszt	*a consequence of absorbing a surfeit of liquid refreshment*
Brown bread	*pate*
Brush your barnet=Barnet Fair	*attend to your hair*
Butcher's=butcher's hook	*look*
Buttons and bows	*toes*
Creamed=cream-crackered	*fatigued*
Currant=currant bun	*sun*
Dickie=Dickie Dirt	*shirt*
Donald Duck	*unsubtle sexual intercourse*
Drop of Rosie=Rosie Lee	*cup of tea*
Drop of Vera=Vera Lynn	*glass of gin*
Easy blag	*fun-loving girl*
Got an 'arry=Harry Wragg	*do you have a cigarette?*
Gregory=Gregory Peck	*cheque*

Half-raspberry=lolly	*half-volley*
Hampsteads=Hampstead Heath	*teeth*
Horse=horse and cart	*fun-loving girl*
Iron=iron hoof	*confirmed bachelor*
Jam-jar	*automobile*
Long hops	*three pints of real ale*
Macaroni pony	*not a negligible sum*
Minces=mince pies	*eyes*
Molly=Molly Malone	*telephone*
Mutt'n Jeff	*hard of hearing*
North and South	*external orifice in head*
Oily=oily rag	*cigarette*
Old China=China plate	*mate* (noun)
On your Jack=Jack Jones	*alone*
Pig's ear	*beer*
Plates of meat	*feet*
Pull the curtains	*move the sight-screen*
Rabbit=rabbit and pork	*converse*
Raffle=raffle ticket	*wicket*
Right two and eight, in a	*in distress*
Round the 'ouses	*trousers*
Rub=rub-a-dub-dub	*public house*
Saucepan=saucepan lid	*kid*
Second hander=second-hand Ford	*Lord*
Shaken by the Jimmy=Jimmy Shand	*a form of greeting*
Smacked the bastard	*hit four runs*
Tea-leaf	*thief*
Thumper	*bat*
Trouble=trouble and strife	*her indoors*

Up the apples=apple and pears	*upstairs*
Wearing an Irish=Irish jig	*sporting a toupée*
Weeping willows	*pillow*
Went for a double top	*touched a lady's breasts*
West enders=West End shows	*toes*
Whitewash, the	*crease, the*
Wilson, the	*wicket, the*
Young Brussel=sprout	*acolyte of Lord Baden-Powel*